FOR

BEVERLY AND VICTOR PASSY

TO MAKE UP

FOR THE OTHER BOOK

MORRIS HERSHMAN

the CRASH of 2086

MAJOR BOOKS • CANOGA PARK, CALIFORNIA

First Major Books edition 1976

Copyright © 1972 by Morris Hershman
Original title: *Shareworld*

MAJOR BOOKS
21335 Roscoe Boulevard
Canoga Park, California 91304

PRINTED IN THE UNITED STATES OF AMERICA

ISBN 978-1-4344-1180-8

1

"Ladies and gentlemen," announced the unseen man with the deep voice, "the President and Board of Directors of the Government of Earth."

There was a moment, surprisingly, during which the vision screen became blank, with a grayish blur that was punctuated by small white bars edging from left to right across every square screen on Earth. The picture suddenly sprang into focus, however, after a white flash like a fireworks explosion.

The faces and half the figures of six men seated at a huge desk could be seen by the camera. The man in the middle suddenly pushed back the largest chair, got to his feet, and walked around the desk and over to a plastic lectern. Behind him and to the left, a multicolored flag could be made out.

"My friends, let me summarize the basic achievements of your government—of your corporation, as it might be called at an annual meeting. And when I have done that, let me give you some indication of how it has come about that histories from now on will take a different tack than they have ever done. I will, of course, be brief."

Gavin Hew paused, his craggy face in a moment's repose, thin lips pursed slightly. Nobody looking at him doubted that he was a forceful executive who would never be an easy man to work for, but who would be fiercely loyal to hard-working subordinates.

"Number one," the President of Earth Government began, raising a lean forefinger. "In spite of inflation, this administration has not raised taxes, nor have we issued more bonds for money to pay debts. Number two: Various government branches have been modernized, making it possible to outlaw violence entirely. I might add that your government has great hopes of solving its current serious difficulties with a certain foreign planet, just as we hope to persuade all members of the galaxy to outlaw war as a means of solving disputes. We believe, too, that we have found the solution to the problem of ensuring the economic well-being of the majority of Earth men and women. Let me take just a moment here to refresh all our memories about how this has been done."

The President paused to clear his throat, and in that moment the vision camera swept across the large desk at the rear of the stage. Seated behind it were the executive vice-presidents in charge of Peace, Agriculture, Stockfare, and Commerce. The men looked uncomfortable and the ample jowls of the Vice-President for Stockfare quivered with annoyance. The camera moved away instantly, back to President Hew.

"In the year 2081, five years ago, when this administration came into office, you will remember, a wave of business bankruptcies was sweeping the planet. You will remember, too, that a number of brokerage firms were behind the failures, because of the many missing stock certificates that couldn't be replaced by those companies. It is not unfair to say that some twenty firms of all types were failing every week.

"Your government chose to set up a central system of stock certificate storage to insure brokerage customers against stock loss. As a result, Earth Government accountants were able to examine brokerage firm books and to order changes or set up mergers when that was considered necessary. I may remind you, too, that the government was empowered to request the courts to appoint trustees for brokerage firms that were considered in danger of failing. The brokerage business was therefore set more firmly on a constructive path, and we all know its great importance to the economy. But then a new groundswell of complaints began to be heard—new and perhaps justified."

President Hew paused to take a drink of water, then folded his hands. He was telling his audience what nearly all of them knew, but he held the attention of every viewer. His sharp eyes seemed to penetrate every corner of every room on Earth in which a vision screen had been located.

"What happened then was simply that different sectors of the population began to protest, having become newly aware that five percent of Earth Government citizens—only five percent—owned the capital that produces ninety-five percent of Earth's wealth. Concerned at this inequity, this administration took steps to remedy matters. Mr. Weaver, our Vice-President for Agriculture, arranged for the distribution of land that had never previously been farmed; this land was to be paid for by government loans. In other words, a new Homestead Act was adopted. Many families formed cooperative units to take advantage of this offer. But not all the poor could be helped in such fashion. The government needed a modern Homestead Act for those poor who live in mobile homes, who own no capital, who have lived off bounties and been denied dignity and self-respect. The government had to launch a campaign to give dignity back to people who'd never had it. How was this to be done?"

Another pause, permitting the camera to be pointed at the Vice-President for Stockfare, who was whispering to the Vice-President for Agriculture. Theodore Carr had been a union leader in his time, and the shrewdness in his eyes made it plain that he was a man of great experience in administration.

"The title of Vice-President for Bounties was changed to Vice-President for Stockfare and a new concept of government was born," President Hew continued with quiet but firm pride. "This government proposed making the common stock of various industries available to the poor. The plan was to give property to the poor—and it is property ownership that gives a man a start toward a feeling of pride in himself. The Stockfare Bureau would insure all credit. Under the supervision of the Stockfare Bureau, local banks would borrow directly from the Reserve and purchase a diversified portfolio of dividend-paying blue-chip stocks for each client. The client, paying off the loan with dividend money, would own the stock outright and could enjoy an income from, say, twenty thousand to fifty thousand credits of invested capital."

President Hew paused again, this time placing his hands palms down on the lectern in front of him.

"This income would not have made a considerable difference in most cases, as this administration was well aware, but we felt that many blue-chip firms would increase their dividends as a result of—um—persuasion. Although the government might have lost money in gathering the taxes of corporations, such money would be largely recovered by increased revenues from personal income taxes. Your administration felt that it had secured a place in world history by this series of moves to solve the poverty problem. We had not, however, gone far enough to solve the new problems of middle-wealth and of wealth itself."

President Hew paused for another drink of water, then wet his thin lips.

"Brokerage firms, many of which had been saved from bankruptcy by the efforts of this administration, began to complain vigorously about our improvidence. I have to add that many middle-income stockholders joined in the complaints. It was the general feeling of these groups that their equities in Earth commerce would be severely diluted as a result of our projected measures. This administration therefore changed its mind about the scheme, but we would never have done so if our economists had not evolved an even more daring scheme. Let me briefly sketch it in."

President Hew lowered his head as if to decide what he was going to say next. It was obviously his own ingrained honesty that had made him remind his audience of these difficulties, and he was finding it hard to restrain himself. When he looked up, his eyes were narrowed determinedly.

"It was the conception of this administration that Earth Government create special 'nonvoting' equities *in itself,* making it possible for the poor to buy those equities on loan in lieu of private stocks. Dividends would depend on the amount of money that could be set aside for such payments. An expensive plan, of course, as dissident elements have not hesitated to point out, but this administration felt that such expenses would be more than offset by the decline in outlays for bounties and for makework activity. (Of course, Earth Government dividends are tax-free.) Once again, of course, the private sector of our economy reacted negatively. And I surely need not go into detail about the way in which these complaints have been met."

Another pause, this time for a direct stare into the camera and then a brisk look away.

"In effect, the complaints have been that the poor would soon be eliminated as a source of cheap labor and ready exploitation," he went on in a voice as strong as when he had started to talk. "But your government continued on its course, aided by the public-spiritedness of such brokerage firms as Grayling's and by the knowledge that we have gained from our experiences in the stock market and what we know about its impact on the economy of Earth. I can say now that this administration has taken the key steps to wipe out poverty for all time."

President Hew looked directly into the camera again, but he wasn't quite as convincing as before. His eyes blinked nervously, his jaw jutted out too far. It was as if Gavin Hew was pleading with the silent and unseen audience to believe what he was saying and not to raise any questions or doubts, let alone pose facts to the contrary. More than one admirer of Gavin Hew suddenly glanced away from the vision screen.

"I would like to address myself to one other major point," he continued, his craggy face becoming less tense with fresh confidence. "It is time to speak to those visitors to Earth who have come to us from the planet Rillut. It is time to speak loudly and clearly, to stress one major point as never before. If my message given in public cannot get through there might even be a danger of—of great difficulty between the two planets, the two mighty powers of commerce. And what I want to say to my friends of Rillut is simply thi—"

The President's eyes suddenly grew wide with astonishment, and his jaw dropped in amazement. He raised one hand in what seemed like an angry gesture, and then the vision screens became gray and blank before going dark. A state speech by the President of Earth Government had been interrupted and the President had been silenced.

2

"Be careful how you put that glass down," Matt Brisbane groaned, cradling his head in his hands, "the noise is bad for me."

"Had a wild night, huh?" his secretary asked sympathetically, although it wasn't hard to guess the answer. "Well, here's something I used to give my husband when he got himself tanked up on Rillut beer. It practically raises the dead and starts 'em snake-dancing."

Matt glanced distastefully at the forest-green mixture topped with red foam. With an effort he drank the stuff, shuddered strongly, and was rising to his full six feet when the visifon on his desk buzzed. He looked at the gray face on the screen, shrugged, sat down again, and put the empty glass inside one of the desk drawers. He drew out a chart sheet and placed it and a pencil ready on his desk. Then he pushed the white button to make his connection.

"Matt?" Jack Armer said. "Are you interested in Preddy-kate? One of our franchisers tells me you've picked up a thousand shares."

"In that case, you know the answer."

"I'm surprised anybody is buying a two-billion-share outfit that predicts the future," Armer said, worried. Then his lips twitched at the corners. "Not for the long haul, I hope?"

"Dow-Jones, no," Matt growled, a little surprised that the top of his head hadn't come off with the volume. "Preddy-kate has been showing a slight rise after a steady fall, so I picked up some shares against the market. I expect I'll get my short during the day."

"That should make you a few hundred credits, I suppose," Armer replied, his eyes narrowing. "You look like you had a rough night."

"I'm all right."

Armer's eyes rested briefly on the pencil and paper on Matt's desk. "I'm surprised you can still work after a big night with some girl."

"My head is pretty straight, you know, Jack," he said, and broke the connection after a few more words. His secretary was still looking down at him, her lined face without expression. Donnet was the widow of a broker who had worked out of Grayling's for many years as the man in charge of the franchise operation of Earth's largest brokerage firm.

"Do you need anything else besides a new head?" Donnet asked. She'd have made a coolly detached nurse in the days before machines had taken over that kind of work.

"So far so good, Donnet," he lied. She turned and hurried out of his small but neat office to her smaller one. Matt pushed two buttons on his desk stock scanner. The market had lost eight points by midafternoon, which wasn't too bad in a market that had broken 3000 only a few weeks ago. Only the Paris Bourse was holding its own during this wave of profit-taking. Matt had always liked that particular phrase, which carried with it the connotation that nobody ever sold at a loss.

He checked the stock scanner again, punching the number symbol for Preddy-kate. It was very slightly down. The stock carried only a million common shares outstanding, which was a low number for stocks in a market where one billion shares per company was closer to the norm. The stock wasn't much good in a market that had in general turned its back on companies that predicted the future. It had finally dawned on some small investors and even on the mutual funds that the price-earnings on future-prediction stocks were too low to justify their prices.

The visifon buzzed again, and the stern features of Euphemia Catlett appeared on the screen. Oscar Grayling's executive secretary didn't want to talk to him every day of the week.

"Mr. Brisbane, you have a clear schedule for the next few days. Isn't that so?"

"Yes," he answered, although he had planned to spend some days and nights with his current girl friend. "That's right, Miss Catlett."

"Good. Mr. Grayling wants to see you. Would six-

14

thirty today be satisfactory?"

"Of course."

The efficient Miss Catlett crisply broke the connection before Matt could say anything further. He rang for his secretary and had just pulled the empty hair-of-the-dog glass out of a drawer when she walked in again. There was a drop of forest-green from the mixture smeared across half the rim of the glass.

"I'm going to need a bucket of this stuff in the shortest possible time," he groaned. "Mr. G. wants me to drop in on him again."

"If you take any more you'll keel over," Donnet answered. "Do you think you'll be getting a promotion?"

"I'll be getting a pain in a more tender area to match the pain in my head," Matt moaned. "I'll probably have to take on some new chore or other."

"It'll keep you away from bad companions."

"But I like bad companions—if they're women." Matt smiled. "Well, I have to suffer for being a bright young man on the way up."

Donnet, who had started to smile, looked at him a bit coolly. "Yes, Matt, I suppose that the hard jobs go to the people who can handle them. There's nothing wrong with that."

"All I want to do is sit under a tree and eat candied yams," he said, sighing theatrically. "When I'm not in bad company, that is."

"I suppose you really do want that."

"Who wouldn't, for Dow-Jones's sake?"

"My late husband never thought of that. He was just an average Earth man who did his best to help raise a small family. All his life he saw the plums go to the smarter men who could sense the way a stock would perform by watching it with their antennae up. Grayling's kept him on the job because he worked hard, terribly hard. He would put in something like twelve hours every day to get done what you accomplish in three or four."

Matt shrugged.

"You've never worked up a sweat in your career," Donnet continued, "and you've already made about one and a half times the money my husband ever made for this firm. You're a very fortunate young man, and I think that you ought to be deeply ashamed of yourself."

He raised his head, jutting his chin out angrily. "For not working twelve hours a day, you mean?"

"No, Matt, for trying to hide your intelligence and doing the least you can."

They stared at each other a moment, then Donnet walked out with deliberate steps, her head high. Matt got up, went to the locker for his coat and a portfolio. He stayed in the office only long enough to arrange the sale of his shares in Preddy-kate and then left.

∞

Outside, Matt walked around the gray building to the rear and then went downstairs to the private tube. As it started to move, he took a chair next to an artificial tree, removed his shoes, and dug his toes into the artificial grass. Several green blades popped off the rug. He bent over and flipped one end of the grass rug over to see if he could find a maker's name. His work for Grayling's had taught him to find out who manufactured any product he came across for the first time. It was a new item from the Samco line. He shrugged and put the rug back in place.

Unzipping the portfolio in his lap, he examined the annual report of a firm that manufactured plastron hearts for transplants. That outfit seemed due for a turndown, its board having added a million preferred shares to the float and sold out a division to—to Samco, as a matter of fact. A mutual fund might want to take a position in Plantron, as the firm was called; a fund would be able to buy so many shares at a clip that it wouldn't need a great upturn before profit-taking. He didn't think there would be much upward movement in an 800-million-share outfit like Plantron without changes in top management.

The tube was passing a poor settlement. Thin children with anxious eyes were playing near a group of mobile homes and unpainted trailers that formed an irregular circle. Tired, lined faces could be seen in some of the windows.

Matt's head began to ache again.

The tube stopped at last and Matt got out. The country air on this warm June day made him feel a little better. The grass and trees were genuine out here, and there wasn't the usual tinny chlorophyll smell that came from special vents. He looked longingly at one of the solid, spreading trees that gave as much as twenty inches of shade, but knew he had to hurry now. Mr. G. was waiting.

As he reached a small tilted-roofed house and stood in front of the door, he heard chimes sound inside. The door opened on Mr. G.'s executive secretary. Instead of greeting Matt, Miss Euphemia Catlett glanced significantly at her watch.

"Mr. Grayling will see you now." She looked at the portfolio in his hand and gave a reluctant nod of approval. "Please come with me."

As he followed Miss Catlett down a long, dimly lit hall, Matt reflected that her figure wouldn't be bad if she could only learn to dress well. He wondered if she had any feelings for or against her boss and whether she had ever been in bed with Mr. G., or indeed with any other man.

At the end of the hall she stepped to one side. As Matt entered a comfortably furnished room, he heard Oscar Grayling saying abruptly, "Take that chair, please, and tell me what you thought of the President's speech."

Matt adjusted the chair back to accommodate his shoulders and rubbed his strong chin vigorously. Grayling wasn't the type to make idle conversation. The grandson of the firm's founder and son of the man who had thought of charging for research on a stock, Oscar Grayling was a small soft-spoken man in his mid-forties whose only interest in life was his business. People at Central Headquarters gossiped that Grayling wanted to be an innovator like his father and grandfather before him, but hadn't yet succeeded in coming up with any new ideas. Business was better than ever, but Oscar Grayling recognized bitterly that his success was produced by rising prices and a well-run firm and not by any unique contributions of his own.

"A pretty good speech," Matt said carefully. He had been at the party that was the source of his hangover

18

that morning at the time President Hew had actually been speaking, but he had seen a summary of the speech's highlights later. "Straightforward, as usual."

Grayling's face twitched impatiently. "Do you feel that the blackout had any special significance?"

"It was probably caused by mechanical failure. Machines fall down on the job sometimes."

"It happened just as he was talking about the Rillut," Grayling persisted. "If the Rillut keep trading as they've done up to now and allow Earth no advantages in its own markets, as I'm sure the President was going to say, our exchange could be driven down to a point where we'll all be lucky if the averages break two thousand again."

"We all know that, sir. Even the Rillut know what harm they might do to Earth."

"Hew was starting to talk about the possible dangers of a war and how he hoped to prevent it." Grayling let out a deep breath. "You know that there are plenty of warlike political elements on Earth and that they'd like nothing better than a good excuse to take off against the Rillut."

Matt nodded. "Just the same, sir, President Hew can get his points across to the Rillut in private. He doesn't have to use the vision screen for diplomatic messages."

"I'm sure he's done that, but he likes to make his major points in an open and aboveboard manner." Grayling folded his hands. "Everybody else feels that what happened was sabotage—I mean the blackout, of course." He was peering alertly at Matt, who shrugged noncommittally.

Grayling nodded suddenly, as if Matt had passed

some important test. "Worse yet, so many people have talked about it that nobody seems to remember something else that happened earlier during the speech and is every bit as important."

Matt cocked his head inquiringly.

"During one part of that speech Hew looked as if he was telling a lie and knew it and expected to be caught out."

Matt started to shrug once more, then winced as his headache surged back in full force. "I'm afraid I can't help on that, sir."

"Not at the moment, perhaps." Grayling's lips expressed disapproval. "And I always took you for a bright young man."

Matt caught himself just short of making a bitter personal remark. There would have been no point to it, though. Grayling wouldn't understand human weaknesses and feelings.

"Weren't you watching when Hew talked about his stockfare program? That's when it happened. I want to know what lie he was telling about the program and why. I want to know if something is badly wrong in Earth Government, and what it might be."

Matt nodded. He could probably find out from one of his government contacts.

Grayling raised a warning hand. "By the way, you're not to put pressure on anybody in the government. I don't want you to start any rumors that have no basis in fact." He leaned back in the chair and closed his eyes. "You'll report when the job is finished, of course. It shouldn't take you too long."

Matt was being dismissed. His lips formed a thin

line as he stood up and reached for the portfolio. "One more thing, Mr. Grayling, if you don't mind."

Grayling looked up impatiently.

"Good evening," Matt said. "I hope you don't mind my taking the time to say that."

3

Matt got home by eight o'clock, flicked the vision screen on, and took his precooked dinner from the portable stove. He was just settling himself comfortably in front of the screen and wondering whether he could work up the strength to call Mitsee, his current favorite blonde, for a night out when the news came on and took his mind off everything but the assignment Grayling had handed him.

"In the state of Russia," the commentator was saying, "two poor men were arrested for disturbing the peace by drinking and carousing. The men, Grigori Tarantzev and Yakov Yoskovlev, were offered a chance to pay their fines with money from Earth Government stock dividends. Each man refused, prefering to spend a night in prison with the threat of a further month's sentence as well."

The screen showed two bearded men being led away by government personnel wearing what the knowledgeable Matt recognized as police uniforms. (The tailors who made all the police outfits had recently dropped their eighteen-percent dividend and there was talk about a forthcoming proxy fight for control of the firm.)

The newscaster started to talk about a Russian ballet troupe. Matt flicked the screen off and turned to the visifon. It was twenty minutes before he could be connected to the trust officer at the Lenin Bank, a slim, effeminate man named Valentin Barzov.

"You're handling the Earth Govermnent stock funds for the poor in Moscow, aren't you?"

"We're the biggest of three banks doing so," Barzov said cautiously, with a smile.

Matt drew his Grayling identification card from his wallet and held it close to the screen. He saw Barzov writing down the number. As he watched, Barzov put through a swift query and received confirmation on a yellow card. He nodded and the smile on his face became broader.

"I want to know if you handle the accounts of Grigori Tarantzev and Yakov Yoskovlev and what the status of those accounts is. The men are on stockfare."

Barzov took the names down, then chuted out the request for information. "What makes you ask, Brisbane? A little out of your line, I'd say."

Matt hesitated. He'd have preferred not to talk about it to Barzov or anybody else just then, but he had to justify his request. He repeated the highlights of the news story.

"If I were in that spot, I'd rather borrow money against my stockfare account than spend time in jail," he added. "I want to know why those men didn't do that."

Barzov shrugged. "Our peasants are not a provident lot, Matt." He glanced at his watch. "Was your market down today, too?"

"It was off ten points at closing."

"Well, you can't say that the market is anticipating a business boom in case of a war with the Rillut." A whirring noise could be heard at Barzov's side. He reached toward his chute door and opened it, drawing out a small slip of paper which he slotted into his magnifying screen.

"We did have both stockfare accounts," he said, looking up after a moment, "but they were closed out two days ago."

Matt blinked. "How can a stockfare account be closed?"

"The men came into the bank, separately I suppose, paid for their stock certificates, and withdrew them," Barzov replied. "That's how."

"These desperately poor people *paid* for the certificates?" Matt's probing eyes made the bank officer half a planet away suddenly flinch. "Each man *paid* for his Earth Government stock with good credits?"

"Excellent credits." Barzov shrugged. "The poor may do as they wish, having purchased the stocks outright. Perhaps they want to make a bonfire of them."

"I see. All right, Barzov. Thank you. I'm much

24

obliged."

"Not at all." The Russian smiled winsomely. "You must visit Moscow sometime soon."

There was no mistaking what he meant, but Matt replied carefully, "I'm sorry, Valentin, but I don't go in that direction."

Barzov's smile had become strained by the time he tuned him out.

Matt frowned absentmindedly over dinner. Even a visifoned invitation from Mitsee failed to divert him from the problem of the two Russian peasants.

Matt disposed of the dinner dishes, his lips pursed in concentration. Then, as if reaching a sudden decision, he put through another visifon call. The face of a short middle-aged man appeared on the screen.

"Ned, I want some information yesterday."

"It's on your desk right now," Ned Jackler replied placidly. He was Grayling's best private investigator. "Refresh my memory, Matt."

"I want to know if a lot of people on stockfare have been pulling their EG shares out of banks after paying for them."

"I can give you a small sampling by tomorrow morning."

"That's good enough."

A trickle of red light into the room told him that somebody was waiting at the door. Matt walked to the hallway, then smiled and hurried to the door to let Mitsee inside. For the balance of that night, to his own surprise and pleasure, he was a happy man again.

4

"Fifty stockfare accounts have been pulled out of the First New York City Bank," Ned Jackler reported over the office visifon the next morning. He looked slightly rumpled and it was obvious he had been working all night. "In each case, the client paid in full for his EG shares and drew them out."

Matt nodded. He was sober but very tired as he tapped a button for the market averages on his desk scanner. The market was down by six points even though trading had started only an hour before.

"Have you got any idea who might be picking up the stock?"

"Uh-uh. And no record has to be made, you know, what with the fourth market."

"I know, but I think I'll hunt around for more information. Thanks a lot, Ned."

Matt waited a moment, then tried to make a new connection on the visifon. Before the circuit could clear he looked at the averages again in more detail. Blue chips were leading the retreat, it seemed, and utilities had tumbled by an average of 5.3 points. It always amazed Matt when utilities plunged. Let a blue-chip utility offer a dividend larger than the ten percent at savings and loan associations or the banks and it would drift around at the same point. But let an untried firm with a wild new product (like a mechanism that would scratch your nose automatically when it itched) offer a new issue, and the stock would climb feverishly even on a bad day. So much for the romance of the market, with hard-eyed businessmen shrewdly deciding where to invest their credits.

The circuit was cleared at last and Matt saw Caspar Krempel's sallow face appear on the screen in front of him. Krempel looked briefly disappointed; he had obviously been hoping the call was from a customer. There were smudgy gray lines under his eyes, and a twitch in his upper lip.

"Have you been doing any business in Earth Government shares?" Matt asked abruptly.

"None of my people have talked about selling or buying EGs."

Matt nodded. Krempel was a fourth-market man who worked by himself. Every morning he'd call each subscriber to his service to ask which stock or stocks that subscriber wanted to buy or sell and at what price. When he found a near-match, a little hard bargaining made it possible for a deal to be struck with a huge block of equities. Neither trader ever knew the other's identity, and the secret trading of so many shares of one firm made it possible to keep the exchange price relatively unaffected. Krempel and his kind were important to the big exchanges now that specialists, who had been needed to keep the market orderly but were always accused of running from a falling market, had been eliminated.

"If you do get a request, let me know."

"Done. By the way, you can do me a favor, too. Have you got any idea who might want to pick up a block of Mary Jane? I've got a seller for six thousand shares."

"No idea." Matt knew that the Rillut-backed firm made perfumed marijuana cigarettes and were embroiled in a scandal because they refused to stop advertising them to the young, for whom they had been proved harmful. "If I hear anything I'll let you know."

Euphemia Catlett reached him on the visifon twenty minutes later. "Mr. Grayling would like you to have lunch with him in his office."

"Twelve o'clock will be fine for me."

"Twelve-thirty, please."

Matt put in an hour's work and then took a shower and changed his shirt and tie for the occasion. A silent elevator took him to the top floor, where the walls were solid glass from top to bottom; one side provided a first-rate view of buildings that were smaller than their predecessors before the United States-China war that had finally led to the unification of Earth.

Over Chicken China, which had become a popular dish now that the war was over, and the long, reddish

Rillut beans that everybody deplored but ate, Oscar Grayling listened to Matt's preliminary report. His thick lips were pursed.

"Somebody is buying EG stocks that were intended only for the aid of the poor," Grayling said. "Have you any idea why?"

"I can guess, of course," Matt answered, swiftly organizing his thoughts. "Somebody wants to embarrass Gavin Hew, and convince Earth that the President has no capacity for helping the poor."

"Who wants to do this?"

"Somebody with money who can unload the stocks, depress prices, and send Gavin Hew into retirement—with the poor people he had tried to help yapping at his heels and poorer than ever."

"And who would that be?"

"Well, the President is certainly a man with enemies," Matt said, repressing an impulse to ask whether he was expected to provide names and visifon identification. "It's even been suggested that the Rillut might be back of this effort to embarrass Earth Government."

Grayling promptly asked, "What's your opinion?"

"I don't suppose it's impossible, sir, that the Rillut are behind all this, but I find it hard to believe. Trying to topple Earth Government is a long way from flooding a market with study groups and offering low-interest loans in undervalued currency on which they've never let a free market set an exchange rate. The Rillut government cuts its business taxes and helps its businessmen form cartels and doesn't let Earth do any business on its planet. No, taking unfair trade advantages is one thing, but trying to break Gavin Hew is a different story altogether. I don't believe it's what they've been doing."

Grayling shrugged. "Better find out the truth as quickly as possible."

Matt didn't need to be told what had to be done. Given the right information, Grayling's would sell out its own stock holdings and gather in its cash. In case of a crisis the firm might need to have more than one credit in capital for every twenty in liabilities.

Grayling waited until he had dismissed Matt with a brusque, businesslike gesture, then showed that he remembered the conclusion of their last talk. As Matt got to the door, Grayling said softly, "Good afternoon."

∞

Matt reached his small office prepared to make more inquires but found a blizzard of notes left by Donnet, most of them from various franchise holders who wanted help from the headquarters troubleshooter. One client claimed that a stock transaction hadn't been recorded properly. Somebody else complained that mistakes in a research opinion about Armasure distorted facts about the book value per share. The GoLight pension fund was skittering on the verge of bankruptcy and so was the brokerage firm of Morgan and Monahan. (The junior partner had lost both sons in the U.S.-China war, and his wife had been killed during a missile raid; he had never been able to concentrate on business again.) Earth Government's intelligence officers were making plans to start their own pension fund and wanted Matt to discuss the plan at a forthcoming meeting. An average day's work, it seemed.

Someday, along with the usual stuff, he would be thanked for doing his job well, but he wasn't going to hold his breath waiting.

The scanner offered no good news. The market was down eighteen points, and though there was some hope that the industrials might stage a rally, nothing was definite.

The stern features of Euphemia Catlett appeared on Matt's visifon. He established the connection.

"Mr. Grayling asks if you are aware of the current happenings in New Washington."

"No, Miss Catlett, I'm not." It never seemed to occur to Grayling or his secretary that even a madly ambitious Matt Brisbane could only be in one place at one time.

"I'll be brief. You've heard of General Domingo Skene, of course."

"Of course." The general had fought for the United States during its futile war with China and had acquitted himself bravely and well. His subordinates often called him unprintable names, but he knew how to get the best out of them.

"General Skene is now in New Washington, according to the latest vision news on screen. He has just interrupted a meeting of the Board of Directors of Earth Government to ask for Gavin Hew's dismissal from the Presidency."

"On what grounds?"

"Overall incompetence, he said at first. When he was criticized for vagueness he said that the stockfare scheme was a disaster that would destroy Earth

Government."

Matt frowned thoughtfully.

"General Skene is still at government headquarters," added Miss Catlett.

"I'll try to talk with him," Matt promised. Before disconnecting the visifon he reached for his jacket, but this time he didn't take his portfolio along.

5

On the way to New Washington, Matt decided that a man like Domingo Skene couldn't possibly have the money to be buying up EG equities. It didn't make the slightest sense that a retired general, however comfortably off, would be able to get so much money together.

Matt knew how small a government pension could be. Before Earth unification, his father had worked for the United States government in an administrative capacity. His income had been enough for comfort but nowhere near luxury. He had been killed in the war and Matt and his mother had somehow managed on his father's pension for the short time before Mrs. Brisbane had also been killed during a missile raid.

But that had all happened long ago. Matt

remembered telling Mitsee how he had felt about his future after both parents had died so suddenly.

"I figured I wouldn't work any harder than I had to," he had told her. "Life is just too short to knock yourself out, so I decided to be a vision actor. Then I tried summer stock and found out what it really means to be an actor."

"I know it's hard work," Mitsee had said.

"I didn't mind the physical work, it was the mental effort. You have to create the character you're acting—how he walks and talks and thinks. If you're not convincing, you fail in front of an audience. I decided to try something else—something not so public—and I wanted to get close to where the money is. That's how I became a troubleshooter on The Street. It's not hard work, most of the time, and I can usually hide my mistakes."

Until the last day or so he hadn't done badly at all. Now, squirming in the tube chair on his way to New Washington, he reflected uncomfortably that if he fell on his face on this assignment every human being on Earth would know about it.

∞

From three blocks away, Matt could see the angry crowd milling around the huge white stone building on C Street that housed Earth Government headquarters, and as he left his rented atomcar, one man was muttering, "We ought to go in there and rip it apart."

"How about half of us going in by the front and the other half by the back?" another man asked. "Then we'll have Hew where we want him."

"Either we get this done now or we forget about it," a

34

hard-voiced man in workclothes shouted. "I'm not going to wait around anymore."

"What the hell *are* we waiting for?" someone else yelled. "There are damn few police inside and I say we don't let this government take the bread out of our mouths. I say we charge in there! We need money and I say we try and get it!"

Matt could see no way to work through the crowd to the huge gates that guarded the building and was drawing back when a man at his side said, amused, "Poor people aren't very smart."

Matt turned. He was looking at a well-dressed man of about his own age. Recognizing Matt as an equal, the man grinned smugly.

"Not as smart as we'd be, no," Matt said, straight-faced.

"Even worse," the man went on, having missed Matt's muffled sarcasm, "they're shiftless and lazy."

"Maybe that's because they are poor. If they could get jobs, they'd work at them as hard as we do."

"No, they'd figure that they have to work too hard for too little money and go back to stockfare and whatever they do to raise a few credits."

"If they owned something they might work as well as anybody else."

"People who own things have worked for them. And don't tell me about the Homestead Act. People had to earn land in those days to survive. These people are given stockfare and on account of a loophole in the law they can cash in their equities and get tanked up on Rillut beer. No, it's not the same at all."

"I still say that giving them property might make

the difference," Matt persisted.

"A matter of opinion, at the very least. I don't agree. Haven't you ever heard how the poor mistreat their children and husbands and wives and even kill them? Haven't you ever seen or had any experience of the stupidity and cruelty and arrogance of the poor? And if they treat relatives like dirt, think what they'd do to property."

"You really hate these people, don't you?"

"Not at all. Being poor isn't fun or graceful or challenging. It's hell, pure hell, and it destroys men and women and children."

Matt was startled. "I thought you weren't sympathetic to them."

"It's not a matter of sympathy. If a person goes mad you have to deal with him within the frame of reference of his madness. You don't say, 'Mr. Jones, the strange man,' but 'Mr. Jones, the lunatic.' Being poor is a form of insanity and you have to deal with it that way."

Matt started to disagree but was interrupted by a cheer from the milling crowd. Matt looked up in time to see the gates to the huge building open swiftly. No one in the crowd made a move forward, however. A flash of metal in the waning sun and the gates had closed again.

As their shouts died down, the crowd parted in the center to let an authoritative-looking man of medium height pass through. Matt could see that he was completely bald and guessed him to be in the fifties although his face was unlined. It was obvious that the life he had chosen agreed with him. The newcomer nodded af-

36

fably at the man who'd been talking to Matt, then moved in that man's direction.

Somebody in the crowd called out, "What happened inside, General?"

"Did you knock off old Hew?"

"What did you tell him?"

Domingo Skene raised a sun-darkened hand, then waited for the silence he knew would follow. "I started by telling the Board of Directors that this administration's pro-Rillut policies would undermine all of us. It's impossible for a man to make a living on earth if some damned aliens are selling their merchandise at lower prices and keeping Earth people out of good jobs as a result of Gavin Hew's policies."

A cheer rose from the crowd. Matt thought that some of the poor looked as if they hadn't worked in years, and then wished that the idea hadn't occurred to him.

Somebody asked, "But what about stockfare, General?"

Skene looked intently at the questioner. "You fought with me at Cleveland, didn't you? Thought I remembered. Laserman first class, weren't you? Yes, that's right."

The man smiled, gratified.

More loudly, the General continued, "I told the Board of Directors that the government had to issue more equities if it wanted to keep a revolution from taking place"—no response from the crowd—"a violent revolution!"

A mild cheer went up, led by his friend's handclapping.

"Now, boys, you know I was mixed up with a little violence myself—before it was outlawed," Domingo Skene continued with mock-modesty, acknowledging the crowd's chuckles with a thin smile. "But I feel that not even the last war, our no-win war, can be compared to what will happen if the poor are denied their rights on Earth. We have to make an end of poverty and if the government won't do it we have to show the Board of Directors that it has to be done—without Gavin Hew, if necessary."

A cheer went up as he finished and marched through the mob. Matt's acquaintance fell in behind the General as he passed, to keep the poor from reaching him.

"But what about us, General?" a man demanded. "How do we convince the Board of Directors?"

"Use your imagination," Domingo Skene shouted back, without breaking stride. "Use stockfare to put pressure on them. Those shares are a weapon in the right hands. They're worth credits, and credits are what this government respects. Use your fists, too, if you have to. Don't be afraid."

Another cheer went up, a stronger one this time. Domingo Skene turned his head briefly to the left and then to the right. He looked smaller than on a vision screen, somehow, but more tense.

Matt moved forward to get in the General's path, but the well-dressed helper deflected him with a shake of the head and an outstretched arm. The General hurried into an atomcar that scooted away from the curb as Matt watched.

He turned back as he heard a somber roar from the

crowd. Half a hundred men seemed to have rushed the gates at the same time, cursing as they tried to batter them down by brute strength. There was a moment's silence as someone called out, badly hurt. The crush against the gates resumed with more fury.

Then the gates opened. The crowd muttered sullenly as about twenty men in brown and blue police uniforms hurried out and began herding the poor in front of them toward the curb. Cursing and shouting, the poor tried to fight back but the police soon cleared the entrance to the gates and sent the last few protesting stragglers on their way.

As a policeman approached him Matt started toward his atomcar but then shook his head decisively and strode determinedly to the huge gates.

6

At the gates he asked to see Theodore Carr, the Vice-President for Stockfare, flashing his work identification card at the visifon screen and announcing that he had been sent by Oscar Grayling himself. Nevertheless, it was early evening before a police guard appeared to let him inside. As he entered, the guard examined the blue-white dial of a machine Matt passed.

"You're carrying metal?"

"Keys."

"Hand them over."

He dropped the keys into a yellow envelope that he labeled with Matt's name. Then he looked at the dial again and nodded.

"Seems like you're clean. Come on with me."

As they waited for an elevator, the guard, a tall, fair man with a wart at the end of his nose, surprised Matt by asking, "You're with Grayling's, huh? Do you know a stock called Vitaman? I got a tip on it."

Matt forced himself to concentrate on the guard's question and asked one of his own: "Who'd you get the tip from?"

"Guy who works for me. I was wondering what you think of that stock."

"I've got no idea what the outfit is or does," Matt told him, "but I think it's a mistake to follow stock tips unless they come from insiders in a firm."

The man waited, his face set sullenly. Matt knew he wouldn't be able to get onto the elevator until he had given the guard some help.

"Do you plan to sell it short?" he asked.

"Uh-uh," the guard said, recoiling as if he had been accused of a crime.

"What's the picture on this outfit?"

"I don't get you."

"What are its price-earnings? What about its competitive position? How many shares has it issued? How strong is the—"

"I don't know about all them other things," the guard answered slowly, "but I think Fred—my friend—said it's got three million shares."

"What does it do?"

"Mostly, they plan to start manufacturing androids."

Matt was internally relieved that he could now offer an opinion, even though it meant shaking his head sadly for a start. "Keep away from android stocks. There are so many humans out of work now that android manufacture will never get anywhere until the Earth picture improves substantially. A three-million-share outfit, small as that number is nowadays, will always be small-credit if it's in a business where the government won't budge to help."

"Fred told me they made a lot of money last year."

"Maybe they did, but by way of nonrecurring income." Matt took a step toward the elevator, walked inside, and turned. The guard was hesitating. "I'll tell you what to do: write down your name and address and I'll get you a look at Grayling's opinion of the stock. If we don't make a market in the damn thing, and I doubt that we do, we'll have an opinion."

The guard nodded, wrote down the information on the top sheet of a pad of paper, and handed it over. Matt supposed that the fellow would buy into the outfit no matter what he was told and by whom; he'd had a tip and apparently that was good enough.

The guard followed him into the elevator at last. A pink flash had appeared on one button in the panel; the guard pushed that button and the light went out. The elevator door closed with a soft squeak, and a pleasant hum followed the car upward. When it came to a stop the door opened on a well-lighted corridor. The guard led the way past portraits of Lincoln and Lenin and Sun Yat-sen. He suddenly turned, a hand raised.

Matt stopped. The guard had turned to what looked like a visifon, but no picture appeared when he pushed the button. Matt forgot his impatience when he heard footsteps along the corridor and saw the girl coming toward him. She seemed sweet and friendly, not beautiful, but the type who could get more than her share of the available men without arousing envy in other girls. She was no taller than five-six, with hazel eyes and reddish hair that fell to her shoulders.

She answered Matt's grin with a polite smile of her own. "Mr. Brisbane, please come this way."

"Are you Mr. Carr's secretary?"

"Sometimes."

"It surprises me that Mr. Carr is able to concentrate on government business long enough to get his work done—sometimes."

She acknowledged his comment by letting her mechanical smile grow a little wider, then turned on her heel. He followed her with pleasure, ignoring the portraits on the walls.

"You could at least tell me your name," he suggested.

"Yes, I suppose I could," the girl agreed, and said nothing more. He wished he wasn't sure that she was smiling even though her back was turned to him.

She stopped in front of a wide white door and tapped softly on it. The door was opened by Ted Carr himself. The former union leader was smaller in real life than he appeared on the vision screen, which he seemed to fill whenever his picture appeared.

"Come in, Brisbane."

The girl stayed outside, Matt realized regretfully when the door closed. Carr looked him up and down.

Matt asked quietly, "Can we sit down and talk?"

"Sure, son, but you won't mind if somebody else listens in."

His first thought was that the girl would hear them

on an interoffice visifon. But Carr led him through a warm anteroom and into a large office with a huge oval desk near the curtained window. There was a map of Earth against one wall and a group of three-dimensional photographs on the other.

Behind the desk sat a man with a craggy Scots face, whose thin lips parted in a small smile at the sight of Matt's surprise. Matt wished his jaw hadn't fallen.

"Mr. President," he said hoarsely when he could talk.

Gavin Hew nodded. "No representative of Grayling's gets short shrift at executive headquarters, especially when he wants to talk business. I'd suggest that you sit down and then we can talk."

∞

"When Skene left this building a while ago," Matt said, having turned down a cigar but accepted a fair drink of domestic champagne from Tashkent (no Rillut merchandise had made inroads here, at least), "He was threatening the government. But I suppose you guessed that."

The President glanced at Ted Carr, who said grimly, "He made plenty of threats at the board meeting, too. He knew that the board can technically suggest a President's resignation, but didn't realize it was very unlikely to happen. He seemed to feel that anything he wanted would be done his way."

President Hew asked, "What threats did Skene make in front of this building, Brisbane, to worry you?"

"He suggested that the poor use their stockfare shares to embarrass the government," Matt said carefully. " 'Those shares are a weapon in the right hands,' were his exact words."

"And what do you think he'll do about it?"

"Try to get control of as many shares as possible and use them to embarrass the government. He'll unload the shares on the market and drive the price down to nothing. These are bad times for equities that pay dividends and are very reliable; when they drop in price they're bought by widows and old people who become disgusted when the steady income buys so little. As for the poor, once they give up their stockfare, the moneys that might have been used for a dividend have to be used to help them in other ways, instead."

"Of course." Gavin Hew leaned back, closing his eyes. "It's a funny thing, you know. We really felt that stockfare was the best way of helping the poor. It never occurred to us to make the stocks nontransferable. It seemed such good business for the poor to hold on to the shares they received that we didn't imagine they would sell out at the first offer and use bread-and-butter money to buy foolish luxuries."

Matt nodded.

"The older I grow, the more convinced I become that a human being has to pay a price for his good deeds, his kindnesses." The President opened his eyes wide. "Or a problem like this one comes about because everybody becomes convinced that government will run smoothly if only men of business are in control and managing it on business principles. Well, perhaps I'm depressed. What were you going to tell us, Mr. Brisbane?"

"Only that I feel pretty sure Domingo Skene is going to make a determined effort to buy up as much stockfare as he possibly can."

"He can't afford to buy up too much of it, you know. A retired general has an income, but it doesn't cover the purchase of millions of stockfares."

"I've thought of that, too, Mr. President." Matt leaned forward earnestly. "Suppose somebody is behind him, though. Somebody with a lot of money."

"Of course that's a possibility," President Hew agreed. "There has to be a man with many millions of credits to spend behind this plan to wreck Earth Government."

Matt pointed out, "If the other side wins, the next administration can simply raise taxes to get back the money it spent in getting rid of you."

Ted Carr, standing with feet apart and rocking back and forth, said shrewdly, "In other words, you think we're in a proxy fight for control of Earth Government."

Matt hadn't put it in exactly those terms, but he nodded as if having expected somebody to understand that much a long while ago.

Gavin Hew sat back in his chair, biting his lower lip thoughtfully. Although he was a more deliberate person than Carr, the zest for battle was in him now. He smiled suddenly, looking less than ever like the dignified and solemn executive whose face appeared so often on the vision screen. It was a winning smile, wide and affably mocking.

"You know, Matt, management has a good many advantages in a proxy fight. To begin with, it can use the corporation's funds to defend itself, to keep itself in office, and in this case, of course, the corporation has considerable money."

Carr, the Executive Vice-President for Stockfare, asked cautiously, "And other programs go by the board, Mr. President?"

"You might say that keeping ourselves in office will have priority until this challenge has been met and defeated." Gavin Hew nodded grimly. "No one will be better off if Domingo Skene becomes the next chief executive. In fact, I'm sure we'd soon be at war with the Rillut. By defeating him in this fight we'll be saving millions of lives."

Carr asked briskly, "But what are we going to do? How do we win?"

"We'll have to wait and see what form the challenge takes and then attack. We can't go out after Skene until we know who else is in his corner."

Matt's face fell. "I guess that is all you can do, Mr. President, except for using publicity to make your points."

Gavin Hew looked up at Carr. "It can be done through your office, Ted. Get that pretty redhead of yours to start the ball rolling."

"Redhead?" Carr looked up. "Lorene Goldthwait, you mean?"

"The pretty one, yes. What she has to do is start the P.R. boys on a campaign to keep the poor from redeeming their stockfare equities."

Ted Carr nodded.

Gavin Hew looked toward Matt, who had made a mental note of the girl's name. "You've been a big help to us, Matt."

"I'm glad I could help, Mr. President," Matt said

with unexpected sincerity.

"Good. And if there's anything else you can do, I'll be in touch."

At first Matt thought the President was just being polite, then he realized that he meant exactly what he was saying. Matt would be called on if it was deemed necessary. And this would be the most important job he'd ever be called on to do.

∞

A guard he'd never seen before was waiting outside for him. As he followed him down the portrait-lined hall Matt kept looking for Carr's pretty secretary, but Lorene was nowhere in sight.

The guard rode silently down on the elevator with him and led the way over to the area where Matt had been searched by the metal-detecting machine and returned his keys. He was turning to go when the guard suddenly cleared his throat.

"You're from Grayling's, aren't you?"

Matt nodded, bracing himself for another query about some stock.

"I once paid ten credits for research on a stock and the advice I got was all cockeyed," the guard growled. "And I think you're wrong about Vitaman, too. It's going to shoot up by twenty-five points at least. And that's just for openers."

"Maybe you're right," Matt said pacifically. It wasn't until much later that he remembered that Vitaman was the android stock the first guard had questioned him about.

As soon as he left executive headquarters Matt picked up a copy of *The Street.* By the dashboard light

48

in his atomcar he saw that the day's market had taken an upturn toward the close of trading and as a result was only down by 11.3. Well, there was hope for tomorrow—as always.

7

Matt's personal stock rose during the rest of the week and that Saturday night found him walking into New Washington's clandestine Club Violence with Lorene Goldthwait. It was a medium-sized room with half a hundred men and women gathered around the bar at one end, and a number at the many small tables. There was a huge sign over the bar that said: ALL PRODUCTS SOLD HERE ARE MADE ON EARTH. Someday someone would explain to him why the lawless elements in a society were often also the most aggressively patriotic, Matt thought.

Lorene and Matt ordered two Russian beers apiece and took a table. Lorene seemed to regret letting Matt talk her into coming. "It's hard to believe that places like this are able to exist."

"The police aren't supposed to know," Matt said, nodding lazily. "I think you'll find it interesting, though."

"I know I'll be interested," she agreed without enthusiasm. "What I don't know is whether I should have come in the first place."

Her eye was caught by a heavy-set man passing by. His cheeks were sallow and his thick lips seemed to have been painted with charcoal. He was clenching and unclenching hard fists.

Matt said impishly, "I'm pretty sure he's part of the floor show."

Lorene, wide-eyed, whirled around to him. "But do they actually—you know?"

"They do, or a place like this wouldn't be running against the law."

He heard a chair scrape on the floor nearby and a familiar, grating voice saying, "You have to get off your high horse or get pushed off instead. What I'm saying is that the government is being run so badly that another chief executive officer is vital to its very continuance."

"Of course, General," another voice murmured.

"And to prove it, anybody who wants to take over the job has got to do something pretty big at a time when Hew is just flopping around. People will remember that, and it'll be enough to make another candidate a front-runner."

"What are you planning to do, General?"

"In this case, I think it's mostly being done for me." Domingo Skene laughed heartily. Matt, turning, saw the ex-General sitting as if at attention during a military parade, piercing eyes gleaming as he glared at his older companion. "With Hew in the executive spot, I hardly have to do anything at all. I'll just wait and bide my time and make it pretty clear that I'm available. And Hew will do it all for me."

"How?"

"I expect some kind of Earth crisis very soon, some breakdown, that will force the Board of Directors to move. A citizens committee can put so much pressure on the Board of Directors that they won't be able to ignore the need for a change."

"Do you expect one crisis to follow another?" Skene's companion asked.

"I think that at least two major crises are in the making right now," Domingo Skene said placidly. "You know how the Rillut are hurting Earth business by undercutting us at every turn."

"Of course I know," the other man said. "An atomcar isn't good enough for my son, believe it or not. He has to have an R-car, the Rillut product. He won't be satisfied with an Earth product."

"I think the Rillut menace will cause a major economic crisis."

"But suppose Hew makes an agreement with the Rillut to allow reciprocal trading on their planet?" the other man asked quietly and carefully. "The crisis will fade away. What happens to your chances then?"

"In that case, I think that pressure right here on Earth will make the difference." Domingo Skene rubbed his hands gleefully. "The poor are certainly going to act up and cause more than enough trouble, either way."

52

"Are you sure?"

"If they don't, I'll stir them up myself. I've always been good at getting men riled up and then leading them in a fight."

The other man said something Matt couldn't hear. Matt turned toward a rigid Lorene Goldthwait and asked, "Have you got some coin credits?"

She gave him three. He hurried out to a visifon booth and called the nearest police headquarters, covering the screen so that he couldn't be seen and recognized. He gave the location of Club Violence, then broke the connection and returned to his table.

"Let's get out of here," he said quietly to Lorene. "I think that General Skene is going to be publicly embarrassed very soon now."

Lorene, who had been looking down unhappily, suddenly stared at him wide-eyed. "What have you done, Matt?"

"I've set up a police raid and they'll be here any minute."

As Lorene eagerly gathered up her handbag, the lights in the room dimmed and a spotlight fell on a raised platform at one end. A roped-off square like a prize ring had been set up on the platform and a flashily dressed master of ceremonies was speaking.

"Tonight, the Club Violence offers another spectacular battle with no quarter asked or given," the announcer shouted as Lorene and Matt started toward the exit. "Entering the ring, James Bertram!"

The spotlight picked out the man with charcoal on his thick lips. He was walking down an aisle only a few feet from Matt and Lorene, raising those hard-looking fists and smiling as he moved. A burst of applause followed him, and a few jeers.

"And his opponent," the announcer shouted, "Chet Holly!"

A huge man entered the room from another direction, hairy arms raised over his head and grinning a salute to the crowd as he moved forward.

"Each of these men has killed two other fighters at different clubs in New Washington and Chet Holly killed a man in this very ring only two weeks ago. As usual there will be an intermission every five minutes and of course this is a no-holds-barred contest—anything goes. And may the best man survive!"

As the announcer climbed out of the ring, Lorene turned to Matt with a shudder. "Are those men actually going to—I mean, is it true? I've heard about this sort of thing, but I never actually believed that they'd—well, you know."

"Yes, they'll kill if they can."

"What are they fighting for?"

"For credits, of course," Matt said, almost brusquely. "The winner's credits are invested by the Montresor Fund—and in some cases, so are the loser's—quite a few fortunes have started this way. Some guys without a brain in their heads have made it big in the market because they were able to kill a man in combat."

Lorene seemed hypnotized. Standing by the entrance, she gazed at the fighters coming closer to each other. Charcoal Lips reached his opponent first, thrusting out a hard hand. Hairy Arms grabbed it and wrenched it, as though trying to pull it off. Charcoal

Lips brought his free hand up to his opponent's neck.

The audience called out advice and encouragement:

"The neck, boy, that's right!"

"What are you waiting for, Chet, an invitation? He's waiting for an invitation! Do it now!"

"Use your legs, Chet, kick him!"

And Domingo Skene's booming voice, shouting encouragement to one of the men, "Make the kill now! Make the kill now!"

Skene's chant was taken up by others who began shouting: "Kill now! Kill now! *Kill now!*"

Lorene shuddered and turned to Matt, looking up at him with eyes that were suddenly filled with pain. "Why do they let this happen, Matt, why?"

Matt touched her lightly on the shoulder. There was no need to explain that in a society without violence, some ghastly outlet was necessary. She must have known it herself. What she wanted, of course, was for him to reassure her that what she was seeing wasn't really as bad as it looked—not as final, not as brutal.

He said, "The Montresor Fund is part-owner of a cement outfit that buries the bodies so that they can't be found." His voice was harsh. "By the time a doctor gets to the loser, cryogenics would be useless as a way of preserving life. It's been thought of, but it's not used. This is elemental, Lorene, life and death."

There was pain in her eyes when she asked, finally, in a voice close to a whisper, "Don't we have to go?"

"Not necessarily," he said, surprising her. "Look in back of you."

There were two tall men in blue and brown police uniforms.

"What are they waiting for?"

"For the fight to be over, so they can come in and make their raid." He smiled tolerantly, his probing eyes gleaming with sad mockery. "Couldn't you guess that?"

"But why?"

"They want to see the fun, too."

" 'Fun'? It's ghastly."

"Yes," he said, as she drew in a sharp breath.

Matt shook his head resignedly, knowing he had wasted his time coming here. The police would make their raid reluctantly, but they'd certainly let Domingo Skene go free. The ex-General was certain to be a hero of theirs.

In the ring, Hairy Arms had managed to clench both fists around Charcoal Lips' bloody neck and was squeezing hard. Charcoal Lips kicked out futilely and then sagged, his tongue protruding from his mouth.

Domingo Skene shouted, "Good, good!"

Matt turned to Lorene. "I think we'd better go now."

She had to lean against him as they walked. A scream could be heard from a woman in the audience just before Matt shut the door.

.

8

Gavin Hew stood up and walked around his desk to welcome his visitor, a tall, regal-looking man with a black, spade-shaped beard. The visitor shook hands with him and sat, accepting the cigar that was offered until he saw that it was domestic. Then he shook his head regretfully, drew out a Rillut-made cigar from a breast pocket, and lit it.

Gavin Hew made no comment. By daylight, the oval desk in his office caught glints and shreds of sun as he sat down behind it and smiled.

"Glad you were in town, Rafe," he said. "It's always good to see you."

"I'm honored, Mr. President," Raphael Montresor said politely. In the back of his mind he might have been wondering whether he had conferred an honor or received one, but he showed no obvious disrespect. "I understand that Earth Government is having even more trouble than usual."

"You ought to know, Rafe," Gavin Hew said mildly, ignoring the multimillionaire's look of wary astonishment. "Several of your funds are getting rid of government bonds and your banks aren't picking up on our T-notes, even for ninety-day periods."

"A matter of business, I'm afraid," Raphael Montresor said regretfully, but he had become more at ease in the last few moments. "Nothing personal."

"Earth Government can use your support."

"And gets it in most matters."

The chief executive officer shrugged irritably. The multimillionaire's support was only verbal and consisted of occasional platitudinous speeches in which he proclaimed that the human condition called for a certain amount of tolerance and spiritual love and compassion, those qualities of which he saw the least in this hard and cruel world. Gavin Hew had once reminded Montresor that pity and compassion were no help either to millionaires or social workers, taking time and energy from the jobs at hand.

"I don't know that I'm getting your support where it counts," Hew said mildly enough. "I need it when the time comes to disburse credits."

"I do what I can," Montresor replied mildly. "After all, I didn't bring the poor into a position of dependence on the government."

"No, but you could help alleviate some poverty by employing more of the poor in your various enterprises."

"Paying them would take more credits than I can afford, Mr. President."

"I'm not asking you to take all the poor under your wing, only some of them." Hew added irritably, "You could surely lend yourself the credits from one of your other businesses."

"Not as many as I'd need to keep those workers on my payroll."

"I think they'd pay for themselves, considering how much extra work you could get out of them."

"A matter of opinion," Montresor said, and drew a deep puff on his Rillut cigar.

"Why, you don't even have servants in your home," Gavin Hew pointed out. "Doesn't your wife need help keeping up such a large establishment?"

"My Tildy doesn't want any servants," Montresor replied calmly. "She's set against servitude in any form whatever."

"Which means that because of her libertarian attitude, several people are being kept from having three meals a day and being able to make a living."

"That's the wrong way to look at it, Mr. President. Our lives wouldn't be made easier if people were hanging around and living off us while all the time they were envying us." The multimillionaire shook his bearded head decisively. "There must be people who want to take over your position, too, Mr. President. Would you want them underfoot without excellent reasons for having them there?"

Gavin Hew felt compelled to agree by shaking his head. It always seemed strange to him that in spite of his power as President of Earth Government, there remained certain wealthy men he couldn't dominate.

Montresor's courteous smile acknowledged the President's unspoken admission of his importance.

Gavin Hew chose that moment to try putting his visitor off-balance. "Talking about being better off, Rafe, I recall your telling me that you've got a controlling interest in a cryogenics firm. I wonder how much better off you think you'll be when the people who consented to be frozen before death are brought back to life and added to the lists of the poor."

"Cryogenics and its consequences are not my problem," Montresor replied, touching his spade beard with a thumb and forefinger. "The firm has agreed not to bring the frozen ones to life until the year 3090. My heirs might be affected in almost a hundred years, Mr. President, but not me."

Montresor had winced. He and his wife had never had children and he was still capable of feeling sadness when some conversational turn of phrase reminded him that he would leave no direct descendants of his own. As Montresor grew older, Gavin Hew had noticed, he seemed to think about it more and more often.

Gavin Hew said carefully, "I've heard you've also got a controlling interest in a firm that hopes to make androids on a mass-production basis."

"I am fortunate enough to own a great many shares of the Vitaman Corporation," Raphael Montresor admitted.

"And I suppose you hope that when you get permission, androids will be used for most menial jobs. You don't care if that adds to the problems of the poor and unemployed."

"I think you can trust me to do the right thing, like any man with a social conscience," Montresor murmured. "Will you clear our firm for mass production, Mr. President?"

Gavin Hew said nothing.

Montresor acknowledged the silence with a grim nod. The multimillionaire would be a dangerous antagonist indeed, Gavin Hew decided, not for the first time. Montresor was no more than forty-five years old, but his fortune had been made many times over. He had capitalized on new issues in fresh technological areas, but hadn't neglected using corporate bonds for their capital-gains advantages. He had milked tax-loss carry-forwards that didn't really exist anywhere but in the minds of shrewd accountants and had parlayed all his holdings into an enormous financial empire.

In light of his wife's inability to give him children, it seemed ironic that the basis of his fortune was a firm called Amniocentesis, Inc., which was engaged in removing possible birth defects from the fetuses of the as yet unborn. This odd circumstance had given rise to many cruel jokes at Montresor's emotional expense, but it was hard to feel sympathy for the multimillionaire, even when he was under great stress.

Gavin Hew continued, "While we're on the subject of business in general, what do you think the market is going to do next?"

"I can only guess," Montresor answered, in words he had often used. "In the stock market you can never anticipate consistently what will happen because most buyers pick up stocks that complement some need in their personalities. Funds, too, are always buying equities that match their images and that their shareholders think it would be prestigious for them to own; after all, the shares that a fund buys are chosen, in the last analysis, by human beings. The human factor is simply not predictable, and nothing else affects the price position of equities. As a result, I can't be sure."

"Do you expect the market to go down? It sounds that way."

"Slightly, perhaps. Certainly until the problem with Skene shows some sign of being settled."

"You can't settle when the other party is determined to fight."

"I agree. All you can do is maneuver him into a situation where he will be quieted."

"How would you suggest I do that?"

Montresor smiled modestly and said in a dreamy voice, "I'm honored to know that the President of EG would ask for my advice."

Gavin Hew let a moment go by and then said quietly, "I'm asking. I'm not begging, Rafe, but I am open to suggestions."

"I would suggest that you give him rope," Montresor said. "Ask for his advice. Call him in for an occasional conference. After all, Domingo Skene's name carries a certain weight."

"You must know his opinion of this administration," Gavin Hew said tautly. "If I offer him a conference, he'll make a point of turning it down in public."

"No, because a man like Skene lives with a sense of duty to a force bigger than himself, a force that you

62

represent at this time. Ask for his advice privately and he'll offer it to you."

"His advice would be the kind we couldn't follow," the President pointed out. "He'd want war with the Rillut, for example. He's got nothing but contempt for people who can't fend for themselves, even if the reasons are beyond their control. His thinking is completely antithetical to mine."

"Give him a job in the government anyway," Montresor suggested, leaning forward to knock off the white ring of ash on his Rillut cigar. "A job that looks big and important, but can be handled by clerks. Put Skene in a distant branch of the government and you shut him up."

Gavin Hew started to shake his head firmly but Montresor warned, "Leave him out and the crisis continues if it doesn't become even worse."

"And what would your position be in that further crisis?"

"I'd go with the market," Montresor said regretfully. "The government bonds in the possession of the firms I control would certainly be sold out and then bought back at lower prices in anticipation of a huge drop. The sales alone would cause such a drop."

Gavin Hew asked softly, "You said a little bit more than you wanted to, Montresor, didn't you?"

The multimillionaire replied stiffly, "I was simply pointing out that in the event of a bad market, I would have to act in the direction my duty to my companies would lie."

Gavin Hew leaned forward intently. "Let me ask you this. Suppose I called on Domingo Skene for his advice in filling high positions in the government with people whose views are in sympathy with his own. Don't you think that there's a very good chance he'd suggest your name?"

Montresor said huffily, "I don't know what you're talking about."

"Don't you really?" Hew continued to stare at his visitor.

Montresor looked away, unable to meet the President's eyes. "Certainly I would be honored by a government appointment if it came from you, Mr. President."

"And you'd have a great chance to work from inside the administration to help Skene."

Montresor stood, his face flushed with anger. "I will not be insulted, Mr. President."

Gavin Hew allowed himself a moment's regret. "We might have been friends for years and years longer, Rafe. Not the closest of friends, but at least there would have been mutual respect between us."

The multimillionaire allowed himself a cool nod before he stood. "You regret what has happened no more than I, Mr. President."

∞

The President's next appointment was an appearance in support of a charity to aid the recently unemployed. Gavin Hew smiled for the vision screen cameras like a man very much at ease and in control. Many of the poor who watched the screen cursed him for smiling so broadly at a time when they were in such serious difficulties. Many others, aware of EG's problems, labeled him mentally as just another hypocritical politician. Most of the viewers waited listlessly for the next news item to appear on their vision screens.

In the meantime, Gavin Hew was arranging a late-afternoon meeting at his office. Ted Carr arrived first, a dead cigar (domestic) in his mouth, which he dropped into a breast pocket just as Tyrell Lofton entered the Presidential office. Lofton was a big man and sole possessor of the political guile the President was popularly supposed to wield on friend and foe alike.

Gavin Hew had started speaking before either man could sit down, Carr heavily, Lofton without a sound. Each visitor listened carefully, Carr's fingers moving as if he wished there was a cigar for him to touch. He muttered profanity under his breath as soon as the President was finished explaining what had happened.

Lofton, severely practical, said, "At least we know who we're up against. Raphael Montresor is putting up the money for Skene's pitch to get rid of this administration."

Carr asked dazedly, "But why in the world does Montresor want to have any part of Skene? He's already got more credits than he could ever spend—I've negotiated some wage settlements with him in my time and I know. He's got power, too. What else does he care about?"

"I'm surprised at your asking that, Ted," the President said mildly. "He sees more business opportunities in a war with the Rillut. That's the only possible reason."

"Well, business might be his field," Lofton said thoughtfully, "but that doesn't mean he knows anything about politics. We'll cream him."

"How?"

Lofton sat back in his chair for the first time since taking it. He was smiling. "We'll take his advice, Mr. President. That's how."

The President's craggy face settled into grim lines. "You'd better explain that, Tyrell."

"Don't take all his advice, of course, but do one of the things he suggests about Domingo Skene. Give him a job."

"In my administration?"

"Of course."

"I'd like to send him away to some other planet."

"He won't go. Besides, we want him right here, Mr. President, where we can keep an eye on him. And, by the way, where he'll have to speak softly. He'll be part of the administration."

"What job do you suggest, Ty? A man of Skene's stature wouldn't accept anything less than a job on the Board of Directors."

"Well, Jim Weaver's wife hasn't got long to live, I understand, and Jim might want to give up Agriculture for a change of scene. We offer Jim the chief ambassadorship to Alpha Centauri."

"Getting Jim away isn't the worst idea in the world," the President said, nodding approval. "But it's a big step from there to putting Skene into that slot. For one thing he knows nothing about agriculture."

"The time it takes him to learn the ropes will be time he's off our backs."

"I don't think he'll accept," Gavin Hew said. "It's such an obvious attempt to muffle him."

The ex-labor leader, breathing heavily, put in, "All he can say if you ask him is that he won't do it. That's the worst he can say."

"He can play the story up on vision screens from one end of Earth to the other."

Lofton shrugged. "Well, if we don't do something fast, Mr. President, this whole business is going to get rougher and rougher."

Gavin Hew nodded. He was damned if he did and damned if he didn't. No matter what else might happen, he might have to spend the next few weeks or months or even years in fighting off a challenge from a man who would be part of his official family. He knew he'd have to do it if only because the alternative might be so much more difficult. His whole life as President seemed made up of agonizing choices.

"I'll have to think it over," he said quietly, turning away from Lofton.

"Of course, Mr. President," the political adviser said smoothly, rising to his feet.

President Hew waited until the door had closed behind the two men at last. Then a curse exploded from between his lips and he reached a hand over toward the executive visifon. With some small relief he saw that the hand wasn't shaking.

9

"And now to continue the vision news," a commentator was saying. "Domingo Skene, the former fighting general of the former United States armed forces, has accepted an appointment as Executive Vice-President for Agriculture on the Earth Government Board of Directors. The move surprised a number of political leaders. General Skene tells the vision screen audience the reasons for his acceptance."

"I know this is going to shock the daylights out of a lot of people, but my life has been devoted to the service of my country and my government. I'll be glad to get back into harness again, and I hope to bone up on the problems of farmers so I'll have the basic knowledge I'll need for this job in just a few weeks."

Matt Brisbane was puzzled as he turned the vision screen down and watched the picture disappear. He could have understood giving a government post to a mutual fund manager or a man from Grayling's, but certainly not to the President's worst enemy.

Donnet came into the small office with several papers to be processed. Matt put one of them on the screen and sighed, "I doubt if this news is going to do the market much good, except maybe in the short run."

"What news?"

Matt smiled up at his secretary's lined face. "You don't follow the vision screen news at all? Lucky you."

"I figure they can't tell me anything I might change."

"Same here, but I have to know what's happening, all the same." Matt punched two buttons on his desk scanner and looked at the figures on a small screen. "The market is rising slowly, but I'll be damned if it's a healthy rise. Do we make a market in Havertrone? It's a conglomerate, but most of the divisions manufacture military equipment."

Donnet nodded.

"We'll have to try to pick up seventy-five to eighty percent of the outstanding shares," Matt said. "They're due for a jump with a warlike character like Skene in the government. The first time he blows his top, we unload the stock."

"I'll get a note on it down to the proper department," Donnet promised as she left the office.

The visifon signaled for his attention. Euphemia Catlett was asking, "Mr. Grayling wonders whether you are aware of the impending failure of Morgan and

Monahan."

Matt blinked. The firm was the sixth largest brokerage on Earth and had recently become overextended by opening offices in Chinese cities and even in what had formerly been a Tibetan monastery.

"I can't say I'm surprised," he admitted.

A small smile of triumph at having caught him unprepared stole across Miss Catlett's stern features.

"Do they want Grayling's to take it over?" he asked.

"Yes."

Matt shook his head. "They couldn't offer us enough money to make it pay."

Miss Catlett's eyes glinted wickedly. "Is that your considered opinion?"

It was a trap, of course. She was going to reveal some new factor as soon as he had committed himself.

"Carefully considered, Miss Catlett, on the basis of what I know now."

Euphemia Catlett's lips pursed primly. "Morgan and Monahan have asked for another government loan, which means giving the government a huge piece of their business. Even Grayling's couldn't compete against EG for business. The firm that gets government backing gets government business."

"If that's true, then the government can support the prices of its own paper," Matt pointed out. "The balance of the market isn't buying as it should. If the government takes over Morgan and Monahan it can use that source to buy its own bonds and T-notes on a ninety-percent margin and pay itself the dividends, or defer payment."

"Do we want the government actually meddling

with other stocks?"

"The government, as largest owner, will have to make a market in certain stocks and will even be buying some stocks for appreciation," Matt pointed out. "That sort of proceeding keeps prices high in general. Grayling's will earn a good profit."

"I'll pass this along to Mr. Grayling."

"Feel free," Matt said wryly as he broke the connection.

He looked at his watch, got up, and left the office, stopping at the door to Donnet's cubicle long enough to tell her that if anybody asked for him she was to say that he was in conference with a mutual fund manager.

Then he walked downstairs enjoying the warmth of this pre-summer day. At the nearest parking lot he borrowed an R-car and drove ten blocks away. Entering a huge building, he took a silent elevator to the fifth floor, touched the doorbell of the first brown-painted door in the hallway, and walked inside. He was in a waiting room with half a dozen vision screens. A gray-haired man in a white smock gestured to him from a doorway.

"Come in, Mr. Brisbane, please."

Matt walked into a brightly lighted room and sat down in a large, soft chair as the man in the white smock washed his hands and dried them.

"You need scaling and a cleaning, Mr. Brisbane," the man said, drying his hands. "Your X-rays were fine. No cavities."

"I always did take a good picture," Matt agreed, hunching down in the chair so that the dentist would be able to work a little more comfortably. "You'd think that with so many new inventions, dentistry would be painless and easy now."

"I wish it were, Mr. Brisbane," the dentist said cheerfully, reaching for his drill.

Matt sighed. At least he had gotten away from all thoughts of business for a while.

But the dentist interrupted his thoughts. "I meant to ask your opinion last time, Mr. Brisbane, about a stock I'm considering picking up. Do you know a firm called Mastro? The product allows you to shut off your vision screen from a distance. I think it's a good idea."

Matt listened patiently, remembering that dentists and doctors were probably the most erratic stockmarket players on Earth. It was rare to hear about a doctor or dentist who put money into a firm that made dental or medical equipment, the sort of firm they'd know very well and from which they stood a chance of earning a profit. Instead they would put their hard-earned money into the most farfetched investments known. Not long ago, the Exchange had helped break up a ring of criminals who were mishandling the investments of medical personnel in a specially created mutual fund. Doctors and dentists always seemed to feel that a long and expensive education that equipped them to deal with the human body also gave them the wisdom of Socrates and the shrewd business eye of an Oscar Grayling.

"Mastro has got two billion shares and has been pretty stationary, which isn't surprising for such a heavy float," Matt said, wondering how to tell the dentist that the stock was a lemon unless it was bought short. If he was wrong, even briefly, the dentist would probably never forgive him.

"I like the idea of being able to turn the vision screen on and off from a long distance," the dentist said, flicking the drill on as Matt opened his mouth. Matt felt relieved by that whirring noise for once, but the dentist, an experienced man, was able to speak clearly over it. "Its pattern is moving up in a rectangular, Mr. Brisbane. I've been watching that stock and making charts, and Mastro looks to me like a—"

Matt suffered in silence.

∞

". . . And now to continue the vision screen news. Former U.S. General Domingo Skene, who recently assumed the post of Executive Vice-President for Agriculture, has demanded more space for his department at government headquarters. Ex-General Skene explains his reasons to vision screen viewers."

"We've got a hell of a lot of things to get done in this department and the more space we get, the easier we can do 'em," the former General announced. "The farmers on this Earth of ours are in trouble. They don't get money enough for their crops and the big farmers are squeezing out the smaller ones. For those reasons alone we need more room to get information so that we can be of greater help to Earth farmers. This department is the farmer's advocate and we have no intention of standing idly by while—"

Matt suddenly wished he owned one of those Mastro vision screen units to shut off his screen from halfway across the room, but he nearly ran the distance to do it himself. Lorene had met him at his apartment for a drink and in a few moments they would be leaving for dinner and the theater.

Lorene, looking attractive in a white dress that flattered her reddish hair and hazel eyes, commented, "He seems to be doing his job."

"I guess he's settling in," Matt agreed dryly.

"You don't sound as if you actually believe that," Lorene said, reaching for her drink. She made a face. "You left out the Rillut peach juice."

He took the drink back from her, grateful for the distraction, then added the liquid. Her hazel eyes were probing his.

"You think something's wrong, don't you?" she asked. "Something about Skene again? You think he's still up to his tricks, still trying to take over the government?"

Matt obviously did not want to commit himself, so she continued, "The news story didn't include this, Matt, but because I work in the building myself I know that Skene has already hired new men to work for him in the extra space he's taken over."

"That's interesting," Matt commented. "Do you know any of them?"

"A few, yes."

"There's a pad and pencil on the cocktail table, Lorene. Write their names down for me, will you? And then we'll have to hurry if we want to have dinner. I've got tickets for the new Rillut play, you know. And from what I've heard about this production, if the Rillut take over Earth theater as they're taking over our trade, we really will be in trouble."

74

10

In his office on Monday afternoon Matt was scanning the monthly economic indicators and the weekly comparisons. The number of unemployed had remained stable, but inventories were up. Personal income was very slightly down, but imports were up. Freight carloadings were up, but exports were taking a bad beating. No surprises, not even from the commodity index, which was carrying on in its usual berserk fashion.

The Rillut figures, which he inspected next, looked encouraging from the Rillut point of view. Matt knew very well that they couldn't really be trusted except for the export figures. He was going over these when his visifon sounded. Ned Jackler's picture was on the screen. Matt swiftly made the connection.

"About those names you wanted me to look up," the investigator said, "I've confirmed all of them and know who they are. I can tell you that everybody whose name was on that list has done investigative work for General Skene in the past."

Matt nodded, his worst fears fully confirmed. "Are you sure?"

"Uh-huh. I know what I'm talking about."

"That's good enough for me," Matt said, breaking the connection. He asked his secretary to put him in touch with Euphemia Catlett and several moments passed before that woman's stern features appeared on his visifon screen.

"Miss Catlett, you have to set up an appointment for me today with Mr. G. It's very important."

"I must know what it's about."

Matt was too impatient to deal diplomatically with Miss Catlett. "No, you must not. All you need to know is that a trusted, high-level employee must see Mr. G.—today."

"All right. I can't promise anything, but hold on."

There was a pause, and then Oscar Grayling's voice could be heard. "Two o'clock will be satisfactory," was the terse decision.

"Yes, sir, I'll be there," Matt promised.

The connection was broken before he could say another word.

∞

The Grayling home shimmered in the late spring warmth. Euphemia Catlett met him at the entrance and without a word conducted him down the long hall to Oscar Grayling's study. The room was dimly lit but he made out Grayling's figure in his usual chair. As he took a step into the room, though, he was pulled up short in surprise. Opposite Grayling sat a male Rillut, his eyes shaded, his complexion and hands painfully red.

Grayling introduced them in his soft but businesslike tones. "Mr. Brisbane, Mr. Yoru-ko."

Matt blinked. "The famous dramatist? I saw your play the other evening."

The Rillut inclined his head in acknowledgment. "I hope you were pleased."

"It was an interesting show," Matt said carefully as he sat down.

"You were not entirely pleased, then."

"No. The acting wasn't to my taste at all."

"May I ask why not?"

"Acting requires depth and not just width," Matt replied, choosing his words with care. "I think that your actors, as Rillut, are very much aware of being disliked by large sections of the audience. They see this problem but not anything else. They can't see the world of Earth people as being one where human beings live and die, marry, and have children. They can't touch their audience but only complain to it, whine to it. That's not my idea of acting at all."

The Rillut was interested. "You have had some personal experience in the theater?"

Matt smiled. "I studied acting at Columbia Academy and later had some work in summer stock."

The Rillut looked impressed.

Oscar Grayling said with a vague smile, "Matt finished his schooling in five years, Yoru-ko. Only five years at Columbia Academy rather than the usual eight."

The Rillut looked astonished.

Matt hesitated, expecting Grayling to conclude the conversation and ease the Rillut out of his study, but Grayling said unexpectedly, "You can speak freely in front of Mr. Yoru-ko, Matt."

Matt couldn't help remarking in surprise, "I didn't realize, Mr. Yoru-ko, that you were so close to Mr. Grayling."

The Rillut smiled. "You mean that a self-absorbed being from my planet was so close."

"I didn't realize that a playwright would also be a businessman," Matt answered diplomatically.

"Rillut people fill many functions," Yoru-ko said. "A Rillut man could be simultaneously a doctor and a factory foreman and it would not be considered unusual on my planet."

"The added training is costly, in terms of production, I would think," Matt pointed out.

"True, of course, but the advantage is that the worker is more flexible by far and develops pride in himself as a workman."

"I suppose—" Matt began.

"There are fewer disturbances of the sort in which a worker says to himself that he is doomed to follow one career until his retirement or death and will never know any other experience. A satisfied and happy workman has a greater variety of choices."

Matt found himself agreeing with the Rillut philosophy. He sometimes wished there was a credits-earning manual skill he could retreat to when his work at Grayling's became too much for him to handle.

"Then you do have another skill besides writing plays?"

"Indeed, yes. I am an export manager for one of my planet's better-known firms. You have perhaps tried Rillut beer?"

"Dow-Jones!" Matt swore. "Who on Earth hasn't?"

There was an uncomfortable pause and then Yoru-ko said, smoothly, "But you still want to know why I am here. I have come to Earth as the unofficial representative of the leaders of my planet who are disturbed by ex-General Skene's intentions."

Matt said automatically, "To become President of EG, you mean?"

"And after that to declare war on my planet. The Rillut trade skills are deeply vexing to many Earth people and such a war would be a popular one at first with the mass of your people."

Matt found himself on the verge of saying that he felt Rillut advantages had been gained in part by unfair means, and were being held by similar tactics, but he was prevented when Oscar Grayling interrupted with a brisk "To business, please. Gavin Hew told me that the government will soon be floating the firm of Morgan and Monahan, and added that he was grateful for the firm's advice. Indeed he asked who else besides myself had advised such a move and I gave your name."

Yoru-ko asked mildly, "Does it not please you to have been mentioned favorably in high government circles?"

"Of course," Matt agreed. "In fact I've come here

with more information about the crisis. General Skene
has hired some men to work in his department, and
I've found out that those men have all had inves-
tigatory experience."

The Rillut playwright was shocked. Grayling
rubbed a hard forefinger over his thick lips. At the
moment he looked very much like his father.

"That means they'll be searching hard for antigovernment material," Grayling said at last. "And they're
certain to find out something that can be twisted to
their purpose."

"Exactly, sir."

Grayling asked, "Do you have any ideas?"

A suggestion leaped into Matt's mind as soon as the
question had been asked. "I think we ought to help
them."

The Rillut grew rigid. Grayling allowed himself to
look briefly puzzled and very unlike his father, but
then a soft smile played on his lips.

"Yes, I think you may be right," he said.

The Rillut started to his feet, but Grayling gestured
him to sit down.

Matt said, "What I was getting at was that I feel sure
we can funnel very special material to the inves-
tigators."

The Rillut looked puzzled, but interested.

"We get in touch with somebody who will forge some
apparently incriminating paper, and when it is found
we allow General Skene's forces to make the most of it
before proving it's a forgery. In fact, we accuse Skene's
people of the crime."

Yoru-ko nodded at last, and even permitted himself

a tentative smile.

"We'll have to use more than one paper," Grayling pointed out, "but I think it could work very well indeed. All we need is Gavin Hew's agreement."

The Rillut looked doubtful. "President Hew is an honest man with no taste for underhanded maneuvering."

"Then we'll have to get this done without telling Hew what's up," Grayling said. "I'll be in touch with Lofton, his political coordinator, before the night is out. It'll be taken care of."

A rare smile lighted Grayling's face as he said softly, "You know, I doubt if either my esteemed father or grandfather ever played a pivotal part in saving their government."

11

"The meeting of the Board is called to order," Gavin Hew began, glancing around the cool, high-ceilinged room. "The first order of business deals with investment counselors, so-called, to the poor. These sharks—"

Domingo Skene was on his feet at once. "Mr. President, I want to protest the order of business."

"—are taking stockfare shares and giving the poor people one hundred shares of inferior stock in exchange, then trading those for two hundred shares of an even worse stock, while telling their customers that the investment is paying off because they have more shares than they began with. It is most important that steps be taken as soon as possible to—"

"Mr. President, I've got a point of order." Domingo Skene cleared his throat, and put both clenched fists on the table as he leaned forward and said, "I believe that the first order of business must be the anonymous letters that every member of the Board of Directors has received in his mail. The antigovernment accusation in that letter is shocking—"

"The matter is on our agenda," Gavin Hew said quietly. "It will be covered before the meeting is done."

But Skene kept talking as if he hadn't heard or couldn't have cared less what else might be said. His head was bent forward, his eyes probing at every director in the room. "This letter accuses the government of using what is called 'full-cost' accounting to turn the cost of exploratory work and research from expenses to assets. This lying and cheating—if that's what it really is, gentlemen; I certainly think we ought to reserve judgment as a matter of courtesy—has to be thrashed out once and for all."

Gavin Hew waited until the former General paused for a deep breath and then said, mildly but firmly, "There are a number of other matters dealing with the day-to-day running of Earth Government which have to be discussed—"

"This matter comes first," Skene nearly shouted, hitting a clenched fist against the shiny table. "Even if the discussion takes until tomorrow or into next week and we all have to go without sleep, we need to know whether our trust is being given to a government whose officials lie and cheat and steal from the citizens, all in the name of—"

Gavin Hew didn't delay. He picked up the gavel and hit its underside against the face of a wooden cup.

"I will not be suppressed," Domingo Skene

thundered. "I will not be silenced!"

Gavin Hew did silence him, if only for the moment, by ordering the meeting adjourned until the following day. He glanced toward Ted Carr. "Come into my office, will you, Ted? And ask Tyrell Lofton to sit in with us."

Domingo Skene was still arguing furiously as the President left the conference room.

∞

The men sat tensely in the President's office. Hew drummed his thin fingers on the desktop without speaking. Ted Carr, too excited to be without a cigar in his mouth even if it was unlit, kept punching his knees with his fists. Tyrell Lofton, who had just heard about the meeting from Hew's taut lips, was sitting rigidly in the third chair that faced the desk and the photographs back of it on part of the wall. Through the window, the June sunlight shone fitfully.

"The charge is phoney," Lofton said firmly. "There's just enough truth in it to make somebody go out on a limb, but it's easy to refute."

"Refute it, then," Hew said. "The sooner the better."

"Maybe we ought to wait until they dig up a whole handful of phoney charges and refute them all at the same time, Mr. President."

"How do you know that Skene's men won't dig up situations with enough truth in them to be twisted around so that we'll be embarrassed?"

Lofton gave a tigerish smile. "We're persuading him not to."

Hew's craggy Scots face suddenly seemed drained of emotion. "I'd like to know just what that means."

84

"We're giving him phoney material so he can pick it up, and when we're ready we'll let him have it between the eyes."

Hew protested, "I wasn't consulted about this."

Lofton sat back without losing any of his alertness, a man ready to spring. "No, Mr. President, you were not."

"The feeling among my subordinates was that I wouldn't go along with anything unnecessarily underhanded," Hew said bluntly. "You were right."

Lofton answered, "I would certainly disagree with the word 'unnecessarily,' Mr. President. This board meeting proves my point about its being necessary."

"If Skene's men hadn't found that particular planted lie, the meeting would have gone forward without a hitch."

"Either that, or they would have planted some lie themselves and brought that up, instead." Lofton was controlling his anger. "You don't suppose Skene cares what material he uses, Mr. President—or do you?"

Hew glanced almost idly at his Executive Vice-President for Stockfare. "I take it you agree, Ted?"

The former union leader slowly nodded, jowls dancing. "I'm afraid so, Mr. President."

Hew turned back to Lofton. "I won't deny that you could be right, Ty. It's perfectly possible. But I happen to believe something you don't. I believe that the government has a responsibility to behave in an ethical fashion, even against somebody who hopes to overthrow it. Now I realize that talk about ethics is old-fashioned and shows a naïve approach to problems of statecraft, but I do believe what I say and want to practice it."

Lofton nodded slowly. "No more plants, Mr. President?"

"None. And I want a conclusive answer about this full-cost business for tomorrow's meeting."

Ted Carr said quickly, "You don't want to come into the board room and admit that the whole business about full-cost is a phoney that Ty planted, I assume."

"Of course not." Hew made himself smile. "I'm ethical, but not suicidal."

"You'll have the conclusive refutation by tomorrow's meeting," Lofton said. "Will there be anything more, Mr. President?"

"No, Ty. And thank you for having tried."

Lofton acknowledged the thanks and said, "If it's played right, you could embarrass Skene so badly as to shut him up for at least a while."

"Agreed, of course. And running a government is a matter of taking care of the day's problems and letting others be handled when that becomes necessary." Hew rubbed his hands together affably now. "We might be able to put a crimp in our friend after all, if we're lucky as hell."

∞

"The meeting of the Board is called to order," President Gavin Hew said, and his glance around the high-ceilinged room avoided Domingo Skene's eyes. "This meeting is a continuation of yesterday's, and the first order of business involves the so-called 'counselors' who are accepting stockfare shares and—"

"Point of order, Mr. President," Domingo Skene said sharply, his hand up. "Yesterday I raised the question of the government's full-cost method of accounting, and I have to insist that the matter be thrashed out before we can hope to go forth—"

"Very well, General," Hew acceded, a small smile on his thin lips. "I have here a letter from the Earth Government Accounting Headquarters, which I believe should explain the matter beyond question. There is a copy here for every director. If Ted will pass them down this side of the room and Norman will pass them down the other side, we can get the matter over in a short time and proceed to other business."

The copies were passed down the table. After a while, the various directors looked up. Gavin Hew asked softly, "Will someone move that the matter be considered closed?"

Ted Carr said promptly, "I so move."

The Executive Vice-President for Peace added swiftly, "Seconded."

"We can now take up the matter," President Hew began.

Domingo Skene was on his feet once again. "Mr. President, I've got a point of order to raise."

Gavin Hew was silent.

Skene, who wouldn't sit at a board meeting when he wanted to talk, stood with legs apart and hands behind his back. "I've had a letter from a government informant once again—nobody else but me has had the letter this time, you'll all be sorry to know. There won't be any chance to decide on tactics to prevent the truth coming out this time."

Hew waited, rigidly motionless.

"It has come to this public-spirited citizen's attention that the government has virtually taken over control of the brokerage firm of Morgan and Monahan," Domingo Skene said. "I don't feel that the government should be so closely involved with a business organization which can be manipulated to its own advantage by the purchase of bonds and other government paper. At the very least the matter ought to be discussed in public. I feel that the business community will agree with my stand when I make that point over the Earth's vision screens, as I fully intend to do before the day is out."

Hew reached for his gavel. "This meeting is adjourned indefinitely." He stalked out of the board room, followed by Ted Carr. It was Carr's friend, the Executive Vice-President for Peace, who phoned Lofton and told the President's political expert to hurry out to the Oval Room because all hell had broken loose.

∞

"What it amounts to," Ted Carr said furiously, stabbing the cool air with his dead cigar, "is that the Board of Directors of Earth Government is not able to hold business meetings because of one man."

"It means, too," Loften added, "that by digging around hard enough, Skene's men can find charges that might be misunderstood by the general public. They don't have to use lies."

"Agreed," Hew nodded. "As I suggested to you only about twenty-four hours ago."

Lofton bit his lower lip, but said nothing.

Carr put in swiftly, "I doubt if Skene'll do much harm with that accusation of his. We got into Morgan and Monahan at this time mainly because of the crisis that he and his backer brought us to; and everyone knows we run an honest government."

Hew said, worried, "If he can come up with a raft of other charges we'd have a hard time refuting, Skene might do us some harm in the long run."

"I can't believe he could," the ex-union leader snorted.

"You're entitled to be an optimist," Gavin Hew said, and glanced pointedly at his political liaison man.

Lofton allowed himself a dig at his superior. "I take it that I'm expected to come up with a workable method for our getting out of Skene's way."

Hew laughed. "I'm not ashamed or abashed at having tried to do the right thing, Ty, no matter what you might think."

Lofton began quickly, "I certainly didn't mean—"

"Furthermore I know as well as you and Ted do that the only way to minimize Skene is to bypass him and that doing it means bypassing the Board of Directors as well. What I need to know is whether or not it can be done, and just how it's to be managed."

Lofton, a little embarrassed, nodded without looking at his superior. "I did some checking on the EG bylaws yesterday, Mr. President, and we can definitely bypass the Board of Directors."

"How?" Carr asked nervously.

Lofton said, "We have to funnel important matters through the Executive Committee. I know that the Committee is only supposed to be convened in emergencies, but I think that's what we've got here."

"Very likely," Hew agreed, then looked up with

narrowed eyes. "The Committee only meets once a week."

"It can meet more often if the occasion warrants."

A small smile touched the President's thin lips at last. "I think we may have got the better of Domingo Skene after all, damn him!"

12

"It's agreed, then, that the function of investment counselor to stockfare clients will be declared illegal," Hew summed up. The three Executive Committee members looked ill at ease in the huge board room. Ted Carr shifted awkwardly in his chair, fondling a yellow pencil almost as if it was a cigar.

"Now we come to the matter of proposals from the Rillut," Gavin Hew said. "They hope to mitigate our antagonism to their trading methods, but I don't see that these new proposals carry us much further forward. A summary is at your places, gentlemen, and I will read aloud, if I may, from the next to last paragraph, if only to help prove my point. It says here—"

The conferees moved awkwardly in their chairs.

Hew, looking up, was suddenly aware of a sound from somewhere outside that filled the room.

"This meeting is illegal." Domingo Skene's voice, magnified many times over and accenting those harsh and fierce tones that suggested profanity without a harsh word being spoken, was demanding, "The attempt to bypass the Board of Directors, to silence dissenters, cannot be allowed to continue."

Hew said tautly, "I can't hear myself think."

The Executive Vice-President for Peace, who sat on the Executive Committee along with Ted Carr and Anthony Potter of Transportation, was holding his ears and swaying back and forth.

"This illegal meeting must stop." The echoes of that much-magnified voice seemed to shake every piece of furniture in the board room. "This meeting is illegal and it must stop."

Carr mumbled, "He'll keep saying that until he knows we've left the board room."

Hew said as crisply as he could, "This meeting will continue."

Domingo Skene's voice called out, "The meeting of the Executive Committee is morally illegal and must be stopped. It cannot be permitted to take away the rights of freeborn Earth men and women."

"Nonsense," Carr sputtered.

The Vice-President for Peace stood up, swaying from side to side. "My ears are splitting."

"We will leave one by one," Hew said calmly, "and we will go down to the basement."

Carr's head snapped up. "You mean that the Executive Committee of Earth Government has got to meet in a hole-and-corner fashion like this? Goddamn it, we're the government."

"The important thing is to make some progress," Hew said quietly before the ear-shattering voice started up once again. "Ted, call Lofton and tell him to go into my office and sit behind the desk until further notice."

The Vice-President for Peace was on his way out of the room, both hands to his ears. At Hew's nod, Carr got up and lumbered out of the room. Hew and the Vice-President for Transportation frowned at each other. Domingo Skene's voice, amplified, rose again with stunning force.

∞

The following Thursday afternoon, Gavin Hew had just finished greeting a political friend—pleasant talks about jousting for office were practically the sole recreation for a president of Earth Government—when his secretary called on the visifon.

"Can you make a moment for Mr. Potter? He says it's most urgent."

The Transportation Vice-President, a large, nervous-looking man with bulging eyes, hurried into the office less than a moment after Hew had agreed to see him. Anthony Potter had done a good job for the government by introducing tube systems in areas that had never known them before and persuading the administration to put up money to introduce car-rent systems. He wiped his forehead with a handkerchief as he entered and then gave the President's hand a firmer shake than usual. He was under great stress.

"What's up, Tony?" The President asked, making his

voice light in order to put the other man at ease. "Isn't The Street buying our Darjeeling airport bonds?"

"They aren't exactly being snapped up, Mr. President, but I wish that was the greatest of my worries." Potter almost collapsed into a visitor's chair. The man's face was whiter than any memorandum page on Hew's desk. "*Our* worries, I ought to say."

"Please get to the point, Tony."

"I—I hate to tell you this but I've got to resign from the Executive Committee."

President Hew, like any man getting bad news, was too stunned at first to react with full force. "Tell me exactly what happened, Tony. Why are you resigning?"

"I—well, I was visited yesterday by Raphael Montresor. He said—many things. The upshot of it all is that he asked me as a friend to resign from the Executive Committee."

Hew raised a bony hand to stop Potter in midspeech, but it was useless. He said finally, "Let's see if I can tell you exactly what happened, even though I wasn't there. Montresor told you that my government won't last forever and that when it's voted out of office and you need a job in private industry, he will see to it that you don't get one unless you resign from the Executive Committee now."

Potter looked down at his hands. His pudgy face had turned dark red. "I'm sorry, Mr. President. In fact, Montresor asked me not to tell you why I was resigning, but just to do it. I felt I couldn't do that."

"That's very honest of you."

Potter looked up, stung by the President's quiet sarcasm. "I'll make it up to you, of course, when the Board of Directors is able to meet again."

"You won't be there."

Potter drew back. "Do you want me to resign from the Board of Directors, too?"

"Of course."

The pudgy man flinched, then said, "I think that would be a mistake, Mr. President, if you don't mind my saying so. I've worked with you for a long time and I deserve better treatment than this."

Hew said, "I agree. But what will happen when Montresor comes to see you again and tells you to start voting against me if you want to be taken care of in private industry?"

Potter looked away.

"You don't belong to yourself anymore, Tony. You've lost the integrity you had when you came into government. For that reason I must have your resignation, effective immediately."

Potter got swiftly to his feet. "I'll draft it now."

"Prepare it at home," Hew said. "Your things will be sent to you."

Potter drew a deep, wounded breath, turned awkwardly, and hurried from the office.

∞

It was late that afternoon and Hew's calender was still crowded. He was in for a difficult evening, too, with another Executive Committee meeting and an appearance at a reception for the Chinese delegation. It was odd, he mused, that the Chinese agreed with him that Earth could thrive in the face of the Rillut threat to trade and commerce. The Japanese serenely felt the same way. It was the French and British and

Americans who were leading the agitation to raise import fences.

The President had decided on taking a short nap at home before the Executive Committee meeting and was just preparing to leave when the visifon summoned him.

"General Skene to see you, Mr. President."

"He has no appointment and I'm tied up right now. Ask the General to make an appointment."

"Yes, sir—" His secretary turned, and her eyes grew wide. "General, you can't go in there!"

Hew was facing the door when it burst open on Skene, anger etched deeply on his face. The ex-General kicked the door shut behind him and stood with feet apart.

"It's time we reached an understanding, Hew," Skene began crisply.

The President, who hadn't been called by his last name unless it was preceded by his title since he had been in office, was startled. It was amazing how the title, the word itself, seemed to protect him, to nourish him, to build a fragile ego.

"If you call the guards I'll make such a damn scene you'll never hear the end of it," Skene snapped as the President leaned over his desk. "Get your damn fingers off those buttons."

"Whatever you want to say, Skene, make it short."

"All right. I know you've been holding Executive Committee meetings and getting things done without paying attention to my charges of corruption on all levels of this government. You're not going to hold them anymore."

96

Hew waited, satisfied to let the ex-General talk himself out.

"Plenty of people know when and where and how you hold these meetings and I can find out and use that special sound equipment of mine. Hell, I'm actually in New York City when I talk to you over that loudspeaker, but you can't get away from the noise. My charges against this government are going to be heard in full before any other business gets done."

Hew said mildly, "You mean that you're going to invent new charges again and again until you can bring Earth Government to a standstill."

"Call it what you want."

Hew looked up as the ex-General turned to leave. He asked coolly, "Do you know what my first thought was when I got up this morning? My first thought was to wish that you were dead."

Domingo Skene turned back, half-smiling now. "And you must have felt ashamed of yourself for thinking it. That's one of the big differences between us. I never feel ashamed." And he slammed the door behind him.

13

Sleep was impossible now, so Hew decided to join his political liaison man in the vision screen room where every day at this time he could be found analyzing a specially cut twenty-minute tape giving political coverage of the last twenty-four hours of Earth news.

Every vision screen in the room was turned on. Tyrell Lofton, slumped in one of the comfortable sofas, seemed oblivious to the jumping images and the babble of a dozen different languages. It wasn't until the President shook him that he nodded, stood, and moving as if under great strain, flicked the master switch that turned off the screens.

"Sorry, Mr. President," Lofton said, looking away as he spoke, for the first time in Hew's recollection. "I was a little upset."

Hew looked keenly at the man, but knew that a direct question wouldn't draw information that Lofton didn't want to give. "I've just had a visit from Skene," he said instead, keeping to business. "He swears he'll keep us from holding any more Executive Committee meetings. We've got to figure out—"

"Mr. President, I'm afraid I can't help you," Lofton said, his voice shaking. "I've been trying to think just how I could say it, but I guess the only good way is to do it point blank. I'm resigning from your staff, Mr. President, effective immediately."

Hew looked sharply at the man. "Somebody's been putting pressure on you," the President said. "Did Montresor tell you that you won't be able to get a job in private industry after my administration?"

"He tried to say that, but it didn't bother me." In a more aggressive tone, Lofton added, "I never let any threats bother me."

"Did Montresor threaten your children, Ty?"

Lofton nodded slowly. "My kids will have to make their own way in time. If Montresor shafts them and leaves word to his successors to keep doing it, my kids might both end up on stockfare."

Hew gave a grim nod in spite of himself. He supposed that violence had been outlawed on earth partly because the power wielders had finally discovered that it wasn't really necessary. Take away a man's chance of ever earning any credits, or, as in this case, his children's chances, and that man was in your pocket.

"I see. Will you be working for Montresor?"

"Not in politics, no, but there's an executive slot available at Amniocentesis and he asked me to fill it."

"Suppose he asks for political advice?"

"I won't give it. I've told him that. I've made it perfectly clear, and he's agreed."

"I see." The President extended his hand, which a surprised and shaken Lofton accepted in a gingerly way. "You know I hate to lose you, Ty."

"Thank you, Mr. President."

"And I'm sure you know that you have a spot with me whenever you want it."

"I'm sorry about all this, Mr. President. I am genuinely sorry."

"You'll be back," Gavin Hew said confidently.

∞

The President sat in his office and stared at some of the papers on his oval desk. Gavin Hew wasn't ordinarily a man to think in terms of being depressed, but he didn't know when his situation as President had ever been more difficult. And now he'd lost his righthand man.

He was in no mood to be summoned on the visifon and wouldn't have answered if his secretary hadn't looked nervous. "Mr. President, I wonder if you could talk to Miss Goldthwait. She's one of Mr. Carr's secretaries and she asked if you might spare her just a minute."

It was the last straw, of course, and the girl was apparently waiting for Hew's explosion. Hew actually took a deep breath, but then decided that nothing good was going to happen today. He had about half an hour before he was due at the reception for the Chinese delegation and so he relented. "Send her in," he said.

Lorene was obviously agitated as she entered his

office, and the President attempted to calm her down. "Sit down, Miss Goldthwait, please," he began affably. "I'm not going to bite your head off, but I hope you'll be brief."

Lorene Goldthwait swallowed hard, then burst out, "Mr. President, people are saying that Tyrell Lofton has resigned. I was wondering if—well, I know this is presumptuous of me—"

"Miss Goldthwait, you're here and there's something you want to say. Why not say it and let me make any decision that has to be made as a result?" Hew added, smiling, "I'm in the business of making decisions, you know."

"All right, then, here goes. I've got a boy f— I know a young man who's very clever. I think he might be able to help with the job that Mr. Lofton did. He really is very clever. He works for Grayling's as a trouble-shooter."

A vague memory drifted into Gavin Hew's mind. "Would he be a tall fellow with a chin that looks like it was made of granite?"

She said, "Matt Brisbane, yes."

"He was here once," Gavin Hew said, and then cocked his head. "Are you seriously suggesting that he be a candidate for Lofton's job?"

"Yes, I—Yes, of course," Lorene responded hesitantly. "I think Matt is shrewd enough to do the job you need done and I hope you'll consider him. I—I don't think you'll be sorry."

"Is there anything else you'd like to tell me, Miss Goldthwait?" he asked gently. "No? Then thank you for having come in to see me. I'll certainly take the matter under advisement."

Lorene ran out of the office without another word. Hew was still smiling when the girl's face suddenly appeared on his visifon. He hesitated briefly to glance at the visitor's chair and the floor and then established the connection.

"Did you forget anything, Miss Goldthwait?" the President asked politely. "If you did, I can't find it."

"No, I— No, I didn't." Lorene swallowed again. "I just wanted to— Well, I forgot to thank you for having seen me, Mr. President. I didn't want you to think I was being—well, being rude."

"Not at all, Miss Goldthwait," he answered. "I know you were under great stress."

This small act of courtesy was characteristic of the man, Lorene reflected. How many men in his position and in the midst of crisis would have given their time to a young secretary in a state of nerves?

∞

The Vice-President for Commerce was the host of the reception that evening in one of the three-story buildings along what had always been known as Embassy Row. President Hew and his wife walked among the people in the huge, brightly lighted salon, smiling cheerfully and stopping every so often for a few words with the guests. He was greeting the Rillut playwright-businessman Yoru-ko, when he was surprised to notice Oscar Grayling in attendance. Parties probably didn't hold much charm for a man whose only conversational gambit was business.

"Forecasts are fine in a bull market," Grayling was remarking to a serene Chinese and a rather severe-looking Australian. "But in spite of the fact that my firm makes good money from forecasts, they simply aren't worth much. Let a stock break on either side and it'll move sharply up or down. That's what the myth says. It might be true if you follow the market by charting, by going for the numbers and getting into a fit when a stock makes an up-tick or behaves, in general, the way you would anticipate. Play the market by following the charts and you cut your losses because you'll sell out pretty quick when a stock doesn't live up to what you expect it to do. On the other hand, you'll make weak speculations, by and large. One of the big secrets of the market though, believe me, is to stick to the method you chose, whatever it might be. Consistency is all. Keep to one method and there have to be times when you'll seem like a genius incar—"

The President called, "Mr. G.!"

Grayling, flattered by hearing his nickname spoken by the President of Earth Government, turned instantly. His right hand was outstretched as he hurried over to the President, a cordial smile on his thick lips.

"I certainly hope everything is holding up, Mr. President."

"If it wasn't," Hew said with a crusty smile, "I wouldn't tell the boss of Grayling's."

He had meant to flatter the man with some small subtlety, but in this case it didn't work. Oscar Grayling stood with a vacuous smile, his mouth open, his eyes glazing over at the need to talk about something that might not directly involve business matters. Hew wondered how this soft-spoken man could possibly hope to exploit the number-one stockbrokerage firm more shrewdly than his aggressive father or piratical grandfather had. One of Grayling's key ambitions in life wasn't likely ever to be fulfilled, he thought.

To help Grayling through an awkward moment, the President asked, "You've got a man working for you named Brisbane, if I remember rightly."

"Matt Brisbane, yes," Grayling answered quickly. "We give him an impressive title, but he's actually a troubleshooter."

"Good at it, I assume."

"Certainly, or he wouldn't have been with us for such a long time. You've met him. I remember his report on it."

"I have, yes." The President looked around, but couldn't find anyone to rescue him from this forced conversation. "Grainy fellow, isn't he?"

"Very much so. He graduated with honors from Columbia Academy in only five years."

"He must be something of a grind." Hew looked pensive. "Large family, I suppose. Your average grind gets married when he's very young so he won't have to take time from his career in order to chase women."

"Not Matt." Grayling chuckled.

"No one to threaten him with, if he's loyal," the President mused, puzzling the other man. Hew cocked his head, tempted for the first time to take the young secretary's recommendation seriously.

"He's been loyal to Grayling's, I'll tell you that much."

The President smiled as if making a joke. "If he can be trusted I might even be tempted to put him on the

Executive Committee."

Grayling's startled response was only to be expected. Hew was well aware that Grayling himself would have been flattered and honored at an appointment to the Executive Committee.

"Brisbane is a good worker, you understand," Grayling said quickly. "I'm not downgrading him, Mr. President, but you have to know one or two things about him."

The President waited while Grayling collected his thoughts. Out of the corner of his eye Hew saw his wife deep in conversation with the frizzle-haired wife of the Vice-President for Commerce. An orchestra had started to play a selection that a music machine would have rendered much more pleasingly, but music machines were frowned on by Earth Government in order to create more jobs for humans.

"Matt Brisbane is a chaser," Grayling was saying. "He's more interested in women than in business."

The President smiled, determined not to seem to take this matter any way but lightly. "If I were his age, I'd do the same. And so would you, I'm sure."

Grayling didn't acknowledge the President's personal comment, but went on, "Another problem with Brisbane is simply that he's bone lazy."

Hew was genuinely taken aback. "Do you mean that a lazy man could climb to a high position in your firm?"

"Brisbane works, of course," Grayling said humorlessly, "but he never does any more than strictly necessary."

Grayling continued talking and Hew, listening to every third or fourth word, gathered that the man really considered Brisbane a good worker, with enough shrewdness to perform well if he received a government job.

"Ask Brisbane to call my secretary for an appointment," Hew decided.

"Of course, Mr. President," Grayling murmured.

The President, turning away, observed Yoru-ko taking a few sips of Earth-made beer and smiling politely at the man who had offered it.

"As good as I have ever tasted," the Rillut was saying with determined good manners. "As good as our own beer." He drew a deep breath, his red face growing darker with the effort, and then put the glass to his lips again. "Delicious. Absolutely delicious."

14

"This meeting stands adjourned," Gavin Hew announced. "Matt, I wonder if you'd stay behind for a moment."

"Of course, Mr. President," Matt Brisbane said.

He stood with the others, but remained in place, towering over his two fellow members of the Executive Committee. He had been rather surprised when the President had asked him to take a leave of absence from Grayling's to handle some political matters for him, but was still astonished at having been appointed to the Executive Committee of Earth Government.

The others filed slowly out, heading back to their offices at government headquarters. To permit government business to go forward in spite of Domingo Skene's attempts to prevent it, the Committee had been meeting at different locations every day.

Matt waited patiently. The President, getting up from a comfortable chair behind a square pine desk, walked over to the window and looked out at the view of New Washington on a wilting July afternoon. He suddenly blinked as the sun's rays fuzzed his sight, and turned away.

"Matt, I wanted to ask how you like your job."

"So far, so good," Matt answered promptly.

"Do you think you can take care of the political liaison work?" Hew asked urgently. "You've been on leave of absence from Grayling's for two weeks now and you ought to have some idea about that."

"I'm pretty sure I can manage it. The other day the chairman for Denmark was asking my advice about whether to make a straddle in shares of Amnerobics. I told him I'd prefer to make a call in that stock in today's market. He visifoned me afterward to say that he wished he had taken my advice. He didn't lose by a put-and-call in the same stock, but he'd have made a mint of credits if he had followed my suggestion."

Hew pursed his thin lips. "I would think that giving out stock market advice might be dangerous in your job."

"No, sir. If I'm right, then I'm a genius. If I'm wrong, it's because politics had put me out of touch with the up-to-the-minute gyrations of the market. In either case, I tried my best."

"What about the Executive Committee meetings?" Hew asked. "Do you think the proceedings ought to be changed?"

"Frankly, Mr. President, I think they're a mess.

Every member of the Committee, including myself, is a political appointee of yours and is grateful to you for the job and status," Matt explained. "He votes the way he thinks you'd like him to vote, taking the side you indicate you prefer."

Hew winced. "What do you suggest I do? If I put political enemies on the Committee—and I would, if there was any chance of getting business done in the best interests of Earth—there wouldn't be any votes at all. There'd be speeches instead, like Domingo Skene's. This administration is fighting for its life, Matt, as you know."

Matt answered quietly, "All I'm pointing out, sir, is that Earth Government isn't being run as democratically as it ought to be. I don't mean what I say as a reflection on anybody's personal honesty."

More calmly now, the President asked, "By the way, Matt, have you been getting any threats from Montresor or Skene?"

"None at all, sir. I suppose they know I can't be reached."

"I was counting on that." Hew looked satisfied. "It wouldn't surprise me completely if we got the better of those two after all."

Matt wanted to say that the fight wasn't over yet, but he held his tongue, thinking he'd been forthright enough for one summer afternoon.

∞

Matt's fifth-floor office at Executive Headquarters was a bigger room than he'd had at Grayling's, but his work was surprisingly close to what he'd handled for the brokerage firm. He was still in the business, after

109

all, of searching out problems and keeping them from spreading.

He was at his desk listening to the latest reports on a killer santana wind in Southern California when his new secretary entered the office with some papers for him to sign. She was a blonde and attractive enough for Matt to wish he had more time for dictation. Ordinarily he kept his private and business affairs separate, but a girl like Nettie Clay made him wonder if it wasn't possible (just this once, of course) to make an exception.

"Any messages for me while I was gone, Nettie?"

"No, Mr. Brisbane. None at all."

"Matt, please."

He was about to get to know her a little better when the visifon signaled for his attention and the handsome features of his former secretary in New York City appeared on the screen. Matt made the connection.

"Mr. Jackler wants to talk to you," Donnet said briskly.

"How are things at the shop? How is Ned doing?" Matt asked. The investigator had taken Matt's place at Grayling's.

"He'll get there," Donnet said, adding, "It'll take him twelve hours to do what you can get done in five, but I think he'll make it."

"I know you'll give him all the help you can. Put him on, now."

Ned Jackler's face appeared on the visifon screen. He looked a little anxious, Matt thought.

"I wanted to ask you something, if you've got time,"

Jackler began.

"All the time in the world." Matt would have walked out on a job before admitting that he worked under pressure. "Before I forget, I ought to tell you that there's been some trouble in Southern California. Whoever has the weather-making contract there is in for trouble and has got a stock with plenty of downward potential."

"The stock is called Wethertron," Ned Jackler answered promptly. "The funds have been dumping it like crazy all day, and its price is already below one hundred."

"Not many takers, I suppose."

"Some, but nobody has to buy at market," Jackler remarked. "They can practically set their own price and get it."

"Do we—does Grayling's make a market in it?"

"Thank heavens we don't. I wouldn't want a crisis so soon on the job." Jackler cleared his throat. "What I wanted to ask is if you know a stock called Vitaman."

"Android makers." Matt didn't have to think too hard. "Raphael Montresor has a big chunk of it."

"Yes, and I'm wondering if Montresor isn't trying to run that outfit into the ground."

"No, I think he's got some high hopes for it on a long-term basis." Matt was controlling his impatience. Fresh information that concerned Montresor was more than likely to be interesting. "What makes you think so?"

"They've issued a very bad earnings report for the quarter, with the per-share earnings down to very little on account of nonrecurring expenses for equipment."

"Does the report clarify that?"

"The report is all double-talk. If we tighten up on restrictions for making reports the company that wants to do it will switch to a different brand of double-talk. Full-cost accounting isn't in the same league."

"Has Grayling's sent an analyst to company headquarters to see what the firm is doing?"

"We've tried, but they haven't wanted to talk to our guy or anybody else we might send out to Siberia. I think that Mr. G. himself made a query and got his head handed to him."

Matt said, "It's not much of a problem for you, as far as I can see. Grayling's doesn't make a market in it, as I recall. Tell the report people to issue a no-news report and buy it short on your own."

Jackler looked patient but tired. "Matt, I was calling to let you know about this. Dow-Jones! I felt pretty damn sure you'd be interested on account of the connection with Montresor."

Matt wished he didn't feel ashamed of himself. He had been so sure that Jackler wanted something from him it hadn't dawned on him that the man wanted to offer help. Somewhat embarrassed, he thanked Jackler for his help, broke the connection, and turned, smiling, to his blonde secretary. "What do you say to some coffee?"

Nettie chuckled. " 'Hello, coffee.' "

"There are sides to your character that I'm not going to like," Matt responded with mock sternness. "And if you can get some croissants to go with the java I won't mind at all."

"I hear and obey." Nettie had begun to salaam when the door opened suddenly.

It was Ted Carr, too preoccupied to notice what might be happening around him. There was a lighted cigar in the ex-labor leader's mouth and the odor made Nettie wince as she hurried out.

"You've got to come with me"—Carr pointed a thick thumb toward the door—"we're going over to Apfel's office."

Matt quirked his brows. Waldermir Apfel was the Vice-President for Peace.

"There's a new mess and I know Skene is behind it." Carr shrugged his mountainous shoulders. "Let's get a move on."

Matt was out the door before Carr was finished speaking.

15

Ted Carr seemed to have aged in the last few weeks, Matt thought as they ascended in an elevator. The cigar in his fingers burned unheeded and he glanced down at it like a man trying to refresh his memory about what it might be.

Waldemir Apfel's office was dominated by a three-dimensional map of Earth that covered one entire wall. Behind a massive mahogany desk sat Apfel himself, a medium-sized man with few gray hairs but a thick nose. Before coming to government service he had been a specialist in business mergers, having helped put together more than one conglomerate; and a well-known labor negotiator as well, making him a special friend of Ted Carr's. At the moment he looked dazed and uncomprehending.

"What do you think of it?" Apfel asked with no preliminaries. "What can we do?"

"I don't know what's wrong yet."

Apfel looked surprised, then glanced reproachfully at Carr and stood up. "Come with me to the vision screen room and you'll see it for yourself, just as I did. When somebody wants to destroy you, there's generally a personal reason. Otherwise you find yourself being blackmailed and maybe making an under-the-counter deal. There isn't anybody in the business world who hasn't been in a position like that at some time or other—"

"Let's cut out the speechmaking," Carr interrupted briskly, "and take care of this mess."

Matt led the way to the vision screen room where his predecessor, Tyrell Lofton, had spent so much of his time. As Apfel sank dispiritedly into one of the deep-cushioned sofas, Carr flicked a switch.

". . . proven without question," Domingo Skene was saying in his usual crisp manner. "The Vice-President for Peace is without question the sole owner of New Washington's clandestine Club Violence, where human beings fight to the death every night. Furthermore I say to you that such underhanded behavior is only symptomatic of a government in which corruption is accepted as a fact of li—"

Matt remembered the club to which he had recently escorted Lorene Goldthwait. He whirled toward Apfel, who was watching gloomily.

"Is it true?"

Apfel shook his head tiredly.

"Tell me yes or no," Matt snapped. "I'll go to bat for

115

you, but you've got to tell me the exact truth. Are you the owner of Club Violence? Part-owner? Did you ever own it?"

"Certainly not." Apfel shuddered. "I did own part of a violence club in Hamburg, but that was back in 'forty-one. I sold out my share and went into more legitimate businesses. Besides, I was an absentee owner. I don't believe I ever went there."

"And you've had no part of any clandestine business since then?"

Waldemir Apfel looked directly into Matt's probing eyes. "Absolutely none."

Matt nodded reluctantly. "In that case, you can forget about it. I'll see that nothing comes of this."

Apfel bit back a question. Carr, not nearly so polite, asked, "How will you handle it?"

"By doing my job," was Matt's crisp reply. He took the sting out of his words with a reassuring smile as he hurried out of the room. "Leave it to me."

∞

Nettie was sipping from a cup as he entered his office. "Have you got time for your coffee now, Mr. Brisb—Matt, I mean? There's a new crisis, I know."

"There's always a new crisis," he said, "but I can always find time for a cup of coffee, Nettie. By the way, see to it that I'm not disturbed," he ordered as she went out. "And—oh yes—I'll be leaving for the afternoon in a little while."

Matt waited until the office door was closed before putting through a visifon call to set up an appointment with someone he hadn't seen for a long time.

116

"Come in, Matt, I'm glad you dropped by," the swarthy man called, crossing the room and extending his hand. "Would you like a drink?"

"Only if it's something domestic."

"In that case, you'll have to make do with water." João Coelho's wide smile showed twin rows of gleaming white teeth. "Or a cigar, of course. I've got some excellent Havanas."

Matt glanced around the room as he took a comfortable slant-chair. An enlarged, framed stock certificate hung on the wall behind his desk next to a photograph of Coelho with President Hew. The wall behind Matt's chair was covered by a huge varicolored carpet he had never seen before.

"This is a symbol," the Portuguese said affably, his eyes having followed Matt's. "It was in the first office I ever had, one which I shared. At the time I made up my mind to own it when I became more affluent, and there it is."

"Yes, you've come a long way," Matt agreed.

His host had started out as a customers man in a branch of Morgan and Monahan, then had made a coup in preferred shares of Fresnon. He had reappeared as manager of the Spacemen's Mutual Fund, trading both directly and off the floor where he could bargain about prices and commission rates with the help of computers and fourth-market men. He had been well aware of stock analyst difficulties in properly rating the value of mutual fund shares, if only because they included the listings from reinvested dividends. After a scandal involving Spacemen's Mutual and two insurance companies, Coelho had become a small-scale importer of Rillut merchandise. Slowly but surely he had built his business position until he was able to come back to the stock markets, but in a new capacity.

"I need your help," Matt began, settling back comfortably in his chair. "I need you to mount a letter-writing campaign to Earth Government. They must be genuine letters from real people, and every one of the writers must state his or her belief that Waldemir Apfel could never own a violence club."

"I'm not certain I can handle that," Coelho remarked. "It would cost many credits."

"I've never thought you would work for nothing."

"All the same, this is not the type of job my firm usually accepts." Coelho drew out a glass from a drawer and filled it with Rillut beer from a plastic bag. "Generally, we send out proxy statements for management during a business year. That is our job, and an honorable one after all."

"Every so often, if there's an added fee, you send out the proxies earlier than necessary," Matt smiled. "It becomes possible to evaluate management's strength with its stockholders, and proxies can be altered after some personal persuasion by your staff."

"Every enterprise has its little tricks of the trade. We are used to person-to-person canvassing when needed."

"Or canvassing in reverse." Matt was smiling ironically. "Was it the Emetron proxy fight where you kept computer tapes with stockholder lists from the dissidents as long as possible and then made them copy the list by hand?"

"I see you remember some of the little coups in

118

which I have been involved. I also advised Emetron how to use company funds to solicit proxies to reelect management. In the Bucklin proxy fight—do you remember that one?—I found out that one of the challengers was a director of a firm in opposition to Bucklin."

"It wasn't true."

"It seemed true, on the evidence that was available to me at the time. I did nothing illegal."

"I'm sure *that's* true."

"Many people searched for illegalities."

"I've never said you don't respect the law," Matt told him. "These days," he added.

"I do indeed. However, there are only certain types of jobs my firm is geared to undertake and the job you request is not among them, I'm sorry to say."

"On the other hand, you wouldn't be far wrong in saying that EG itself is in something of a proxy fight now and if any further need for your services were to come up, I would certainly keep you in mind."

"I see," Coelho said after a pause. "If this job is done well, then I may count on your good will in getting further government work. This is what you're telling me, Matt, isn't it?"

Matt waited.

"In that case, yes, I shall certainly make the attempt." Coelho glanced at the timepiece on his right hand, then got to his feet. Matt also rose but didn't offer his hand. He had made an agreement but preferred to keep Coelho at a distance.

Coelho flushed but forced a smile onto his face. "You didn't even take a cigar when I offered it, Matt."

"That's right, I didn't," Matt agreed, and walked out of the office.

∞

"And all these letters have arrived," Gavin Hew was saying on vision screens Earth-wide, pointing to a huge mound of envelopes. "These letters are proof that an overwhelming number of people believe the Vice-President for Peace, Waldemir Apfel, to be innocent of the foul charges made against him—as indeed he is. There is documentary proof of his innocence as well, and I herewith offer that proof."

It was early August, and Matt was in the vision screen room with Ted Carr and Waldemir Apfel himself.

Carr let out a deep breath. "We'll wait five minutes, then go in and tell the President that he's proved his point beyond question. I'm damn glad this is over. It's been a grueling few weeks."

"Yes, but we handled it," Matt said quietly, "and we'll handle whatever Skene and Montresor decide to pull on us next."

"Do you really think they'll try anything else?" Apfel was startled. "We've beaten them at every turn."

"I don't think they're as upset by that as you might be," Matt said carefully. "Their strategy is never to leave us alone—to put up new and different challenges every time we turn one challenge aside. They want to make us punchy."

Carr asked warily, "Don't you think they're succeeding?"

"Not yet."

Carr looked at his timepiece, then tucked his unlighted cigar back into a breast pocket. "We have to go in and see the President, and congratulate him on the visicast."

Gavin Hew was wiping his lean face with a royal-blue handkerchief when the three men entered the warm, garishly lighted studio. At the far end of the room, two men with shovels were doing android work, easing the mass of letters into twin laundry carts; Executive Headquarters, following a Presidential directive, employed human beings for even the most menial jobs.

Hew looked questioningly at Matt as he approached.

Matt nodded reassuringly. "You did fine, Mr. President. I think that'll hold them off for a while."

The President rubbed a prominent cheekbone. "Not for a long while, I would think."

"No, sir, probably not."

Ted Carr winced. Waldemir Apfel shrugged tiredly.

A door opened at the far end of the room and Lorene Goldthwait hurried in, saying, "I'm sorry to interrupt but this is marked 'urgent and confidential.' " She handed an envelope to her boss.

"Thank you," Carr said. He glanced at its face, but didn't open the envelope. "A social matter, Lorene. I was expecting this."

She nodded and walked out, closing the door behind her. The President turned to his Vice-President for Stockfare. Like Matt, the President had been struck by the sudden flatness in Carr's usually vibrant tones.

"Anything I should know about, Ted?"

"I assume so, Mr. President. It comes from Domingo Skene. I recognize that sprawling handwriting of his."

121

"Tell me what's in it."

Carr opened the envelope clumsily. His eyes raced over the contents and when he looked up, his lips were taut at the corners.

"Skene is asking for a special meeting of the Board of Directors of Earth Government," Carr said. "The purpose, Mr. President, is that of demanding your resignation."

In the pause that followed, Matt made a point of being the first to speak. His voice was self-possessed, as if nothing was really wrong or unexpected. "They never get tired and they never leave us alone."

Hew nodded. Matt saw that the President, whose skill at business infighting had made him a legend before he accepted his present high office, looked drawn. "We have to fight him again." Determination gave a steely edge to his tones. "And we'll give him a damned good fight."

16

"The Rillut are a bunch of wild animals when it comes to business and you know it," Domingo Skene was saying loudly. "They go from one territory to another with their goods, selling at lower prices than the locals and making trouble. The sooner they get chased off Earth, the better."

"That would mean war," the Vice-President for Commerce said carefully.

"Half a dozen men can get together with a few grenades and run them off Earth. The Rillut won't shoot back."

"Their home government would declare war," insisted the Vice-President for Commerce.

Skene glared around the conference table. "All those who didn't come out here just to flap their tongues put your hands up. I want to know who's with me and who isn't."

Before anybody could respond to the ex-General's harangue, Gavin Hew said quietly, "This meeting is now called to order. As there is no agenda for the board today, I believe I am justified in declaring—"

Skene got to his feet. "I called this meeting because I want you to resign," he said bluntly. "You've been a rotten traitor from the start and you're damn well going to ruin Earth if you don't step down fast."

"You mean because I won't send us to war with the Rillut?" Hew's calm self-possession contrasted strongly with Skene's belligerence. "You won't be satisfied until Earth commits suicide and you can be the leader of the last battalion."

"The Rillut have only a few bombs, and not much else."

"There will be no war during my administration," Gavin Hew said firmly. "Now about this special meeting—"

"War is not a dirty word," Skene broke in furiously, leaning forward and pounding a fist on the table in front of him. "You always talk against war because people get hurt and killed in it; and that's an unfortunate byproduct, of course. But didn't you ever stop to realize just how much civilization owes to war? The only reason the industrial revolution ever got under way at all was to tool up for war. Without it there never would have been the medical discoveries and conveniences you take for granted in everyday living. War is responsible for your comfort and safety, so you might as well face up to it."

124

"We don't need to go into—" Gavin Hew began.

Skene wouldn't be stopped. "There isn't a large entity of government—not even this one—that wasn't built up by war, and it's the big states that have the money to support business groups that push science ahead and that help the arts."

Ted Carr burst out, "Civilization through disaster, is that what you mean?"

"Look at the facts," Skene snapped. "Whatever Earth has achieved in government, science, and art, it owes in large part to the institution of war."

Matt found himself thinking there might just be some truth in what the ex-General was saying. Certainly it was arguable. But he didn't know how much truth and didn't think he ever wanted to find out. He was beginning to realize why it was that men could have followed Domingo Skene to their deaths: It was impossible not to be swayed by his complete belief in what he said and sometimes in its grotesque plausibility.

Hew rapped on the table to bring Skene to order. "I think we can proceed to this point: if there is no business for the m—"

"Yes, there's business," Skene snapped. "I want you out of the Presidency because you're not running a democracy anymore. You've turned Earth Government into a dictatorship. You get two or three of your cronies together and you all meet secretly and call yourselves the Executive Committee. There's no discussion, no democracy. If EG isn't democratic anymore, if the other side can't be heard, then the current president has to be kicked out."

Matt was silent, struck by the hopelessness of it all. Skene and his friends wanted to overthrow the government, but were outraged if the government tried to defend itself. Skene's group wanted to use any means at hand, but its members couldn't understand that the administration's defenses, if this fight was kept up for a long enough time, would have to become more and more stealthy and less and less on the right side of the law. It was always the unscrupulous dissidents who demanded righteousness from their enemies.

"I don't see any agenda for this meeting," Hew announced, exactly as if no one had spoken. "Without an agenda I don't know what we can hope to accomplish here."

Skene took a deep breath. "All right, I'll give you an agenda. I've got here a study of the workings of this government"—he reached into a plastic portfolio and drew out a thick file folder—"which was commissioned by the Better Government Group, headed by no less a businessman than Raphael Montresor himself. I might tell you that it is very critical of the way Earth Government is being run by this administration."

Hew said flatly, "I don't see what we can do about it here."

"The least you can do is to set up a study committee to report back on it."

"I don't think you understand my position, General." The President was smiling now. "What I have been trying to say for the last few minutes is simply that according to our bylaws and our constitution, no matter can be discussed at a special meeting unless it appears on the predetermined agenda."

Domingo Skene pounded the table as if to crush it. "You knew in advance what this meeting was about."

"It was called as a courtesy to you," Hew answered. "I thought there might be some item on a previous agenda that you wanted to discuss."

"I want to discuss getting rid of you," Skene shouted, his face purpling. "I demand we put it to a vote."

"I'm sorry, General, but as no such item appears on the agenda, it cannot be discussed at this time."

Skene said hoarsely, "Put it on the agenda."

Matt leaned forward to whisper to the President, who had briefly hesitated. Hew nodded and Matt leaned back.

"At your request, General, the item will be put on the agenda, but only for the next regular meeting." Hew paused icily. "In the emergency circumstances under which we're living, of course, I don't know when the next regular meeting will occur."

Skene controlled himself with difficulty, his lips tightly compressed.

"Is there any other business from a predetermined agenda for this special meeting?" Hew asked. "No? Then I declare this meeting adjourned. Do I hear a second? Thank you, Ted. All those in favor—"

∞

Matt parked the comfortable R-car—no Earthmade vehicle had been available—in a secluded, treeshaded area. By the time he had opened the door on his side, Lorene was efficiently taking out the picnic basket and walking to a shady place where she could sit down with him. Matt hauled the picnic hamper of liquids over to that area, a hamper whose contents were almost evenly divided between Rillut and Earthmade products.

"That looks like hard work," Lorene said cheerfully as she busied herself at unwrapping the contents of the hamper she had carried.

"I've been doing plenty of hard work since I got to this town," Matt answered, half-jokingly.

Lorene's hazel eyes were on him. "Are you sorry I recommended you for the job you've got?"

"I'm sorry about it pretty often. I've said that before."

"But not sorry all the time?"

"Well, not right now."

"Do you really feel angry about my having suggested your name to the President?"

"No, not really. It makes an interesting change."

She looked quizzically at him. Matt tried to distract her by pulling out his pocket stock-market console and punching a few buttons to learn the day's averages.

"Leveling out," he observed. "It's amazing that big buyers have to go by the pace set for them by the Exchange, where the little guy deals in the market, by and large."

"Where the little guy loses his shirt," Lorene amended primly, reaching for the salt.

"He doesn't have to," Matt said. "Anybody can make a mint in the market if he only follows the basic rules, even though everybody has heard about exceptions. To make money over the long haul, though, you have to be consistent."

"What are the other rules?" she asked, her head cocked skeptically.

"The most important is not to put all your eggs in

one basket," he said, smiling as Lorene drew out three eggs from the heater compartment. "What I mean, of course, is that you never ever risk money you can't afford to lose. What's more, you put some of it into savings after every successful deal."

"How does a buyer make successful deals? That's what I want to kn— Wait, I can guess. He follows some other rules. Does he have to be what you call a chartist, somebody who studies price movements of stocks?"

"What you have to be is consistent, Lorene. If you want to study stock charts, fine. If you'd rather examine stock growths and profits, past performances and current competitive position, the overall state of the economy and its marking picture, the management strength and the earnings and p-e ratios, that's fine, too. But don't do one thing one time and another thing another time. Above all be consistent."

"Suppose you're a chartist and you get a hot inside tip," Lorene persisted. "What do you do then?"

"You never follow a hot tip unless it's from an insider." Matt made his voice stern, almost as if he hadn't said the same things in that same stern tone of voice to any number of other girls who had been fascinated by the notion of earning money in the stock market. "Be very careful whose hot tip you follow."

"All right, suppose I know what I prefer to study," Lorene prodded. "Once I've bought a stock, though, I haven't got the slightest idea what to do with it."

"I agree that you have to know in advance the way you should handle a stock," Matt nodded, salting the top of his hardboiled egg. "Basically, and assuming you've bought for appreciation, you've got to know when to sell. That's much easier than you'd think. If you've got a loss, take it fast and get out; if you're ahead, run the profits up and as soon as a slide is under way, get out. Don't hang on waiting for a stock to come back or you'll lose your shirt—your blouse in this case, and very pretty, too. If your stock goes up and you think it can do even better, buy more. If it goes down and you're stuck with it, don't buy more. Don't average down, just get out. That's all you have to know, Lorene, that and the simplest rule of all: Pick a stock whose movements you'll be right about beforehand."

"You're a great humorist," Lorene said flatly.

"There are a lot of small points that go with the big ones—for instance, that you should never think of a stock as having a personality and by that reasoning become attached to it. A stock is just a piece of paper and it might make some credits for you if you play it right. Nothing more or less. It's not an extension of your personality, a prestige item, or a Rorschach test."

"If I know all the rules, then I assume that other people know them, too," Lorene said carefully. "It might happen that if I'm following a rule and buying some stock, somebody else who probably knows the same rules is selling it."

"That's a matter of the personal element, of people getting attached to a stock. No matter what your experience has been with any stock, somebody will take it off your hands if you decide to sell. In the old days that was known as the Greater Fool theory, but it doesn't indicate what the guy who sells you the stock might think of *you*, Lorene."

"With advice like that, it's a wonder the President

ever has any troubles at all."

"Gavin Hew isn't following one of the basic rules," Matt remarked. "Hew is letting his opposition run him and not vice-versa."

"You mean that he should quit the Presidency now with trouble on the job?"

"No, but he should call the tune and set the standard. I'm saying that Hew should set the challenges for his opposition to crack, that he should lay down the gauntlet and bring his opposition to him."

"How?"

"What he might do, for instance, is—" Matt smiled, then suddenly leaned forward and kissed the surprised redhead on the cheek. "You're wonderful, baby. You're the brightest girl I've ever been with. I think the President is going to get a pleasant surprise when I talk to him next time."

17

Gavin Hew sat in the small room that was unfurnished except for two chairs and a row of benches along the walls. It was the last week of August, and he was impatient to escape the depressingly humid atmosphere in such close quarters. He shuffled the papers in his hands impatiently.

Matt Brisbane, sitting next to him, said, "As soon as we get the signal, Mr. President, you go out there and pour it on."

There was a rap on the door. Matt opened it on a long, well-lighted corridor and found two bodyguards waiting for the President. In the distance he could hear a burst of applause and some footstamping as well as whistling and cheers.

Hew nodded in the direction from which the applause was coming. "They're on my side," he said comfortably, but added thoughtfully, "I think the crowds were a damn sight more eager in Belgrade last week."

As the President walked onto the stage, the applause grew louder. Matt ducked into a side room, where a vision screen had been placed on a table that looked as if it was made of gutta-percha; Matt made a note of the manufacturer's name before reminding himself that he didn't work for Grayling's any longer.

He saw Gavin Hew advance to a mahogany lectern at the center of the stage and set his papers down. The crowd went wild.

"My good friends," President Hew began, his voice firm and clear. "You are the farmers, you people in this audience—some of the farmers to whom this administration gave land in an attempt to ease our current unemployment situation. Apparently, in your cases, the attempt has been successful."

More applause and cheering and foot-stamping. Matt saw small smile-crinkles appear around the President's eyes.

"There are other men and women, other families, who have not been able to receive land that could be worked. There are the aged and infirm, the very young and their mothers. For these people, your government has adopted the measure that has come to be known as stockfare, in hopes that—"

Matt knew that the President's remarks were now losing him his audience as an epidemic of coughing and whispering spread through the crowd. The entire New Paris Coliseum was expressing its displeasure with stockfare without demonstrating crudely. These

133

people had been helped, but were saying that Earth Government shouldn't help others. Matt winced and wondered bitterly why a decent and capable man like Hew stayed in Earth politics at all.

Hew cut short the further remarks about stockfare that he had intended to make; he had had a similar experience in Belgrade the week before. "In summary, then, your Earth Government is faced by many challenges, my good friends. None of them is more difficult than that which is posed to us by the trading policies of the representatives of the planet Rillut."

A jeer went up, probably at the name of the hated aliens who were outproducing Earth and cutting prices for their products.

"I feel, my friends, that a number of points must be made clear to the Rillut people and their representatives, as well as to certain native elements on this planet of ours," Hew said carefully. "I am aware that there has been talk about war against the people of Rillut. It has been said crudely that war would advance the higher interest of humankind and also that it would put a great many faltering business firms on their feet once again. We know that the fifty major companies on earth own half of all this planet's manufacturing assets. Twenty-three large banks have their own representatives on the boards of three hundred out of five hundred major companies. It has been said that these major firms, acting on the economy, control every citizen's health and safety, and place considerable pressure on Earth Government to conform with their wishes."

There was a scattering of applause this time. Hew

134

looked directly into the vision screen cameras.

"I want to point out that the government has hopes of putting through legislation requiring that all corporations be chartered by the government and that conglomerate corporations be made illegal. The economy would then be ruled by true competition, by free competition. Companies would be of a size consistent with managerial capabilities. In such legislation might lie the hope of Earth citizens for a better life."

Matt smiled grimly. This speech amounted to throwing down the gauntlet with a vengeance. It was the second time that President Hew had made this same point in a public speech, and Matt supposed that Raphael Montresor, among others, must be grimly furious.

"But much of this is perhaps beside the point," Hew continued. "It has been said that business, as presently constituted, requires that war be declared periodically by the government in order for business to flourish. That is not true, my friends. Business can flourish without such artificial stimuli. There will be no war between Earth and Rillut. There will be negotiation, not war."

Another cheer this time, longer and almost loud enough to make up for the volume of badly controlled malice that had emanated from the New Paris audience at Hew's favorable mention of stockfare.

"Earth Government has outlawed violence in all its forms and will not practice it," Hew continued after a pause to sip water from a silver-rimmed glass that had been set down for him on the lectern. "I wish to say, too, that Earth Government has always felt tariffs to

135

be harmful on a long-term basis, but that we may be forced to put some tariffs into operation here, if the Rillut will not modify the unfair currency and trading practices which have done so much to cause unemployment among citizens of our planet."

The speech wouldn't run much longer, Matt thought, and as he went out to the corridor to meet the President, he heard a final burst of applause. Hew, his craggy face bathed in sweat, paused to shake hands with an important local dignitary before walking quickly off the stage.

As Matt approached him, Hew was smiling with grim satisfaction. "That's it," he said. "I think our friends know they're in a fight to the finish this time. Let's see what they'll do about it."

In only six days, during the first week of September, they would find out exactly what the enemy's plans were.

∞

As the overhead light beat down upon the unconscious man on the operating table, Dr. Sidney Duntzer talked as much to himself as to the assisting nurses and technicians.

"Certainly can't use a P.T. on this fellow," he murmured. "No partial thickness graft when you work with the facial area—I could scar the man for life. It's amazing how little thought most patients give to an operation like this. They rent a car a lot more carefully."

Duntzer was a big man with thick brows and oversized ears that could hear a jaw drop, as the hospital staff had often remarked. Now he frowned as one of the nurses muttered something under her breath.

"If you're not feeling well, Miss Crane, you may leave."

"There's nothing wrong with me, Doctor," the nurse answered, her rabbit-like nose twitching. "It's just that I hear something funny, like a ticking noise."

"*I* don't hear anything," Dantzer said shortly, shifting his attention back to the patient. "This is simply a job of using skin the way somebody else would use facial makeup. Someday there'll be a makeup that smooths away operation scars for years and years, so that a plastic surgeon won't have to be bothered with these youth-maintenance cases. Yes, yes, here we are." He gestured with two fingers, then looked up angrily. "Nurse! You should have been ready with the hovoscope as soon as I signaled. If you make one more error, I'm going to have to ask you to leave the amphitheater."

"I'll be more careful," Miss Crane said, her rabbit nostrils twitching as if she had been struck.

"See that you are," Duntzer snapped. "A man's life and happiness could depend on it."

"Yes, Doctor." She passed a needle and transparent syringe filled with an aquamarine-colored liquid to the gloved doctor. There was a pause. Duntzer's skilled hands probed the patient. The needle was moved to strategic points on the patient's face. Duntzer stood back, scowling.

"Are you sure that was the correct bottle?"

"It must be," the nurse said, her face whitening in fresh agitation.

"The patient's color doesn't show the response it

should. Take that bottle and make sure it's—You've broken it!"

"Doctor, I give you my word that it was an accident. I didn't even have a chance to look at the label just now."

Dantzer gestured brusquely to another nurse. "Miss Bancroft, please. Attend to it."

"I'm terribly sorry, Doctor, but the label can't be made out anymore."

Duntzer sniffed the liquid, keeping his eyes on the patient. "That doesn't smell right. Crane, you've done quite enough."

"I'm terribly sorry, Doctor," the nurse apologized in a frightened voice. "I can check out the cabinet contents, though, instead of waiting for the computer list afterward."

"It might be too late by then. Crane, you're excused."

Edith Crane protested, "I guess I was distracted by that noise. I don't know what it is, but it's still going on."

"Nobody else hears it; and your care certainly hasn't helped the patient." Duntzer turned away and began issuing careful instructions to the operating team, telling himself that the precautions should minimize any ordinary damage.

If something unusual didn't happen to go wrong—well, Duntzer told himself, he'd cross that bridge when he came to it.

He came to it unprepared, very suddenly and swiftly. There was a flash of light, obscene in its brightness, and a horrible noise. Duntzer and the staff knew no more. Miss Crane, who was fatally injured, survived for two days only because she had been on her way out of the room. As for the patient, he had known nothing for a little while before the operation began and he never knew anything else again.

18

"The bomb couldn't have been made on earth,"
Domingo Skene said clearly and carefully to his large
and angry audience and to the others who watched on
their vision screens. The ex-General stood with feet
apart in his usual belligerent stance, head just a trifle
forward, eyes gleaming as if they had been freshly
shined. "We know where the bomb must have been
made and we know who probably made it. This was a
Rillut maneuver, a criminal act to explode a bomb in a
hospital and take the lives of—"

∞

Matt was waiting with Ted Carr to confer with the
President. Carr, his usual cigar forgotten as if it had
never existed, paced up and down his comfortable
office.

140

"Skene and company did this, didn't they?"

"I'm pretty sure about that. The nurse said she heard ticking noises before the blast. Rillut bombs are noiseless until they go off. You can bet that bomb was made on Earth."

"How are we going to handle this?"

"I'm not sure just yet," Matt admitted.

Carr glanced curiously at him. This was the first time since taking this job that Matt had admitted that he didn't know how to cope with a crisis. He looked older than his twenty-six years now, hardly the same man Carr had met such a short time before. . . .

∞

When Matt got back to his own office, Nettie Clay told him that Oscar Grayling wanted to make contact, and Matt activated the visifon. This time there was no trouble from a subdued Euphemia Catlett and in less than two minutes the soft-spoken owner of Grayling's was visible on Matt's screen.

"You know how the market is responding to this new crisis," Grayling began in his abrupt fashion. "How do you suggest we play it?"

Matt, forgetting his own troubles and Earth's for a moment, nearly smiled. The older man had got into the habit of asking Matt for advice and kept doing it in spite of the change in their relationship.

"I don't know," he muttered absently, "I simply don't know, Mr. G."

Grayling's eyes widened in surprise. This wasn't the Matt he knew. . . .

∞

Domingo Skene stood up to shake hands with the

visitor to his New Virginia home, a small pudgy man with a sprawling moustache and sideburns, who was accompanied by an even smaller woman, evidently his wife.

"Good to see you, Layton," the ex-General said. "We haven't fought together since the battle of San Diego—no, San Francisco. Right?"

"Yes, sir," Layton said. "I—well, frankly, I can feel my trigger finger itching again."

"I don't blame you for wanting to kill at least one Rillut," Skene said firmly. "It's time we proved just how tough we Earth men really are."

He led Layton and his wife down a hall lined by a display of war trophies and into a large dining room. Half a dozen men waited to greet the newcomer, men he hadn't seen in a long time. Layton introduced his wife, who was greeted only by a few nods and several raised eyebrows.

"Let's get moving," Skene said. "This is a small punitive expedition, to show that the Rillut can't take Earth lives and get away with it."

The woman protested, "But you can't—this could start an interplanetary war."

"If war should happen, and with cowards like the Rillut it's hardly likely," Skene said, not looking at the woman, "Earth soldiers will give an excellent account of themselves."

After this rousing speech they moved out, Layton glaring at his wife, who had insisted on accompanying him.

Skene demanded that the group use R-cars, and Layton, in the third and last car with his wife and a man named Perkins, had imagined he would travel in the General's car, at least. But the General had looked at Mrs. Layton, small but determined, and consigned them to the rear. As if making a sudden decision, Layton rapped a foot furiously on the car floor, then turned away from the line of cars.

"What's wrong?" Perkins asked. "Why aren't we going in the same direction as the General?"

"We'll get to him later, Perkins, just you and me. First, we have to drop off my wife. Otherwise we'll never even get near the action."

Mrs. Layton looked furious and Perkins could only fume as they lost sight of the others and moved in the direction of the nearest private home. Mrs. Layton got out in grim silence. Layton's last sight of the woman he had married was of her standing on a curb shaking both fists at him.

Layton pushed the speedometer to its limits, but by the time they reached New Washington and the Rillut building on Avenue G, it seemed that the punitive expedition was over. Layton and Perkins were vouchsafed one unforgettable view of Domingo Skene, his arm raised as if he were clutching a sword and gesturing fiercely at the only car that was following him.

"Follow me, men," he cried. "Let's drive these damn cars into the damn building and burn the Rillut out!"

19

Matt was sitting with Ted Carr and the President in what had at one time been called the War Room. A huge map of Earth covered an entire wall and a number of visifons rested on the two long tables that ran down either side of the room. There was other equipment for communications, most of it in gleaming chrome so bright that it hurt Matt's eyes.

The President, breaking a visifon connection, reported, "They're trying to ram their R-cars into the building—as if they hadn't done enough damage already."

Carr, who had entered only a moment before, asked, "What damage, Mr. President?"

"They ran over and killed an Earth man who had done a lot of work for the Rillut visitors," Gavin Hew

144

answered tonelessly. "A man named João Coelho—the first victim of their senseless violence."

Matt could respond to this fresh shock only with a numbed sense of agony.

Ted Carr urged, "Surely Skene's use of violence against Earth people will turn his followers against him."

"They will only care about what he does to the Rillut. I've already been in touch with Premier Emmi-to but he may not be a strong enough leader to prevent his people from declaring war."

Carr persisted, "What's to be done about Skene?"

"We've sent the police out with orders to stop him by any means."

"Any means short of violence?"

"Any means at all," Hew said grimly. "The stakes are so high that if we have to use violence to get him, we will." He added, "We should have heard something by now." He began to pace restlessly. Then, decisively: "There's no more time to waste. I'm going on the vision screen as soon as possible to promise a full investigation of the so-called Rillut bombing and the Skene violence. I also plan to promise full and complete protection to every Rillut on Earth," the President went on. "That ought to have a certain calming effect, and it might give Emmi-to a chance to be more of a statesman."

There was silence in the room until the visifon summoned Hew again. The President took the call with the aid of an earphone to insure privacy and though it was impossible to see his face as he listened, his shoulders drooped eloquently. Hew broke the visifon connection with a slamming motion and turned to Matt.

"The police and Skene are in direct confrontation now," he said soberly. "No result yet."

Carr said belligerently, "I'm almost glad his intrigues are in the open. If war with the police is what he wants, let him have it."

"But how many people are going to die because of him?" Matt snapped. "Can't you hear what you're saying?"

Carr bristled angrily but Hew quieted him with a hard hand. "This is no time for fighting among ourselves," he said. "We've got to concentrate on my statement to the people."

∞

Hew sat back, read what he had written, then sighed. "Short, but effective. Investigations and protection promised and that's all. The first statement I've made for a long time in public without mentioning stockfare."

Matt answered with the first remark that came into his head. "Promise the people you'll issue more stock. In that case, Montresor will have to spend a fortune to buy the stuff, and the more he buys the more you'll issue."

"What was that?" Hew demanded.

Matt said carefully, "I was just thinking that we might water the stock, that's all. Montresor could pay for his own downfall, so to speak. It was intended as a joke, Mr. President."

Hew regarded him thoughtfully. "Exactly what you're saying isn't practicable, of course, but what we might be able to do— Well, never mind for now." He

146

looked at his timepiece and reached for the papers in front of him. "You get your best ideas at the worst possible times, Matt," he added, leaving the room.

"What do you suppose he's got in mind now?" the ex-union leader asked.

Matt was saved from trying to answer when the visifon sounded. It was the police report on Skene, at last. The ex-General had led what proved to be his last charge, slamming his R-car into the Rillut building. He had been followed by two men in a second car who were apparently part of his task force.

"Is Skene dead?" Matt asked.

"Yes."

Matt nodded. Earth was safer without him, but he was going to miss that brave, charismatic monomaniac.

"The men in the second car were also killed," the police guard added. "Both cars caught fire."

Matt was tense now. "Did the fire spread?"

"I'm afraid so. It got to the Rillut building and just about turned it into a shell. We've recovered half a dozen bodies so far, one of which we have been able to identify as a Mr. Yoru-ko. That's all the information we have at this time."

Matt was saddened by this personal loss. Yoru-ko had been a Rillut of great dignity and high intelligence. Matt was afraid of what effect this incident would have on Hew's promise of full protection for all Rillut remaining on Earth, and what the reaction would be on the planet Rillut.

Matt broke the connection and turned sadly to Carr. "The President must be told."

147

"The President is visicasting right now," Carr answered. "I wrote out the message so he'll get it while he's talking and revise his speech."

"That's fine," Matt said with tired approval. "After all, why should we keep the good news to ourselves?"

"A preventive war against the Rillut has become a necessity," Ralphael Montresor was saying into a vision screen camera. "As the leader of a group calling for better government, I feel that Earth will not rise to a new level of happiness, a new era of peace and plenty, until the members of the planet Rillut have come to realize that they have declared economic war on us, and that they cannot be allowed to do so with impunity."

The vision screen announcer said softly, "But President Hew will not declare war."

"In that case, Mr. Hew must be forced out of office for the greatest good of the greatest number." Montresor reached into a pocket and pulled out a piece of blue paper. "I have today sent a demand to the President of Earth Government and his Board of Directors, calling for the subject to be put to a vote at a regular meeting of the Board, at which I would be invited to appear. I feel that such a meeting is crucial and that a declaration of war against the Rillut must be discussed and voted upon once and for all."

∞

Matt leaned back on a sofa in the vision screen room, a small smile playing on his lips at sight of the multimillionaire making his grandstand play. He got to his feet slowly and walked to the Mastro to turn off the screen. He was still smiling as he left the vision screen room and walked down the hall. The sight of him drew an astonished glance from Nettie Clay, who wasn't used to seeing her boss so much at ease at a time when everybody else was living under intense nervous strain.

Matt reached for the visifon as soon as he got to his office. The President couldn't be reached. He hesitated for no more than a second more and then got in touch with Ted Carr.

"Ask the President to see me as soon as possible," he told Carr.

The jowly Vice-President for Stockfare looked cautious, his eyes narrowing. "More bad news?"

"Not this time," Matt said cheerfully. "I think the President ought to be told that Raphael Montresor has just put his head in a noose."

20

Gavin Hew, on his way out of the office to a meeting with several experts on the Rillut question, looked impatient when Matt came in. And he remained edgy when Matt had told him his idea.

"You want me to hold a special meeting where it can be photographed for the vision screen, and you feel that I should tell Montresor exactly what I think of him and why and that the whole Board will repudiate him. Is that correct?"

"Yes, Mr. President, it is. The Board—"

Hew said brusquely, "I haven't got the time or the inclination to take part in an empty charade."

Matt blinked, astonished to hear a man bred in business and matured by politics talking heatedly against what he chose to call an empty charade.

"Especially not this time," Hew added. "Not when my negotiations with Emmi-to of the Rillut are going forward."

Matt asked, "Could we call the meeting and then not have you or the board appear? Let the vision screen audience see a multimillionaire in a complete state of frustration. Let him be driven to saying things he'll regret afterward. You don't like dishonesty, and this would be a chance for the vision screen audience to see a ruthless and arrogant man as he really is."

"Very well," Hew conceded, gesturing Matt toward the door. "I'm already late for my meeting and there are some people I want Ted Carr to meet."

Matt left the President's company and was on the way back to his office before he asked himself why the Stockfare Vice-President had to be introduced to a number of experts on the Rillut question. Like so many men who prided themselves on their honesty and straight dealing, Gavin Hew could fasten on some secret and not let out a word until the hinges of hell froze over. Matt told himself that he might be in politics forever but he would never understand a politico as long as he lived. He pulled himself up short. With a good job at Grayling's to get back to, there was no reason to stay in or near politics for long.

∞

Nettie Clay wasn't in sight, so he called Lorene into the office and put her to work contacting the Board members on the visifon.

Ted Carr had already been briefed to stay away from the meeting Matt had proposed to the President, but the Vice-President for Peace wanted to appear and knock down Montresor in full sight of millions watching on their vision screens. Matt finally talked him out of it.

He found more difficulty in persuading Ali Nedim Olcayto around to his way of thinking. The Vice-President for Commerce was relatively new on the job, and edgy about missing a meeting that had been scheduled.

Narendra Basu, who had made his fortune through arbitrage and fourth-market dealings, was concerned about the fluctuation of at least one stock he held and could talk about nothing else.

"I own five thousand shares of Preddy-kate," the Vice-President for Transportation said, his voice agitated. "Why does a stock always go down in price after I buy it?"

Matt shrugged; nowadays he found himself being asked for advice about stocks as often as he ever had been. People took it for granted that he had taken some magical secret with him when he left Grayling's and that he was now at liberty to disclose it.

"I can try to get some inside information on Preddy-kate for you," Matt said cheerfully. "And I'm sure I can count on you not to show up at tomorrow's Board meeting, as the President requests."

"Yes, yes, yes," Basu sighed. "That damned Preddy-kate!"

Matt made the other contact swiftly and received the promise he wanted. Having finished the calls, he took a moment to glance out at the balmy September weather and turned back to a pensive Lorene.

Her hazel eyes were gazing seriously into his. "If

something goes wrong at tomorrow's meeting, we might have war with the Rillut," she said quietly.

"Nothing will go wrong."

"But if it does, Montresor could plunge Earth into a war we couldn't win."

Matt turned to the girl, who looked calm and sure of herself, not at all the way she had looked when he had taken her to the Club Violence. He wondered if the day-to-day crisis atmosphere in which she worked had done something to mature her.

"Yes, a disaster is possible," he admitted quietly, not minimizing the seriousness of a situation for the first time in talking to her.

"Thank you for being so honest. In that case, we have to try our best to make sure nothing goes wrong."

∞

The Board meeting was scheduled for one-thirty the next afternoon and at a quarter past one Matt received a visifon from Ned Jackler.

"Some news you might want," the former investigator began. "Our multimillionaire friend has been making some stock transactions this morning."

"Montresor always makes deals of one sort or another," Matt said, careful not to let himself look overly interested. "Why are these new ones different?"

"These are fourth-market deals on a person-to-person level," Jackler said. "Montresor has just bought five thousand shares of Preddy-kate from the Vice-President for Transportation. The stock isn't very good and the Preddy-kate bond issue isn't doing any better than their preferred, but Montresor bought five thousand shares of common at a price that's ridiculously high. Basu has got himself a nifty profit."

A muscle tightened in Matt's cheek but he said nothing.

"Any other deals?"

"Five thousand shares of Ovaltor from Ali Nedim Olcayto. I know as well as you do that Ovaltor has been bankrupt for years, but Olcayto has just turned a very good profit."

"Any more?" Matt asked, concealing his anxiety.

"Two others, yes. Do you want details?"

"Not right now," Matt answered. "Thanks very much, Ned. I appreciate this."

He broke the contact and got in touch with the police guard in front of the building. "This is an order. I want you to make sure that no member of the Board of Directors is allowed into this building today."

The guard protested, "I'm sorry, sir, but the members of the Board have already arrived and been admitted to the building."

Matt's voice became more urgent. "Do you know what Raphael Montresor looks like? You mustn't let him—"

"I'm sorry, but he arrived with Mr. Olcayto," the guard broke in.

"Thank you," Matt said mechanically and broke the contact. He fairly ran out of his office and up to the visicast room, where the Board meeting was to originate. A guard stopped him at the door.

"Break up that meeting immediately," Matt ordered.

"Can't be done, sir, except on the highest authority," the guard said. "The Directors are waiting for Mr.

Hew."

Matt ran back to his office and picked up the visifon. He couldn't reach Ted Carr but he did get through to Waldemir Apfel, who accepted the contact almost instantly. Matt's heart was pounding.

"That Board meeting has to be stalled some way," he said. "I haven't got that much authority, but maybe you can swing it."

"I'll take care of it immediately," Apfel answered.

Matt hurried down to the vision screen room, where he discovered a tense Ted Carr sitting with Lorene and President Hew. The President was staring at one of the screens as if he couldn't believe his eyes.

Ali Nedim Olcayto and Narendra Basu were looking respectfully at a self-possessed Raphael Montresor. Suddenly, Hew saw, Apfel walked authoritatively onto the scene. The Budget Vice-President, Watslaw Jeroscz, looked up guiltily as Apfel entered.

Matt whispered, "I didn't expect him to go in there."

"He'll do whatever he can," Hew answered.

"I'm going to get into this brawl, too," Carr snapped. "Apfel is outnumbered."

"It's better that way," Hew pointed out. "Let the public see how Montresor will act toward Waldemir. He'll try to take advantage of him as he would anyone else. Let the public decide about Raphael Montresor. That's what we all wanted in the first place."

Matt nodded reluctantly as the President glanced at him for confirmation, but it took all his self-control to sit down calmly and even manage to cross his legs. Lorene's skeptical eyes noted his tension, of course, but the girl said nothing.

155

The Board meeting, as they saw on the vision screen, began at the stroke of one-thirty. Raphael Montresor spoke first, his voice thinned and raised in pitch by mechanical reception, the words almost painfully clear:

"The President hasn't arrived yet, so perhaps we should get the meeting under way."

Apfel said stoutly, "We cannot begin without the Chief Executive Officer."

Montresor responded carefully, "In my opinion—and a quick check of the rules will probably show I'm right—there is a quorum now that you're in the room, Mr. Apfel."

Waldemir Apfel's face appeared drawn. He started to raise his body from the chair, but a glance at the vision screen camera made him sit down heavily once more.

Narendra Basu said, "I move that the meeting be called to order, now that we have a quorum, and that I preside. This meeting is crucial and it must go forward."

A number of cries of "Seconded!" were heard above one "Opposed!" from Apfel.

"Motion carried," Basu said. He rose and walked to the head of the table with an odd shuffling motion, and sat down, clutching a number of papers.

"May I speak?" Montresor asked, his black spade beard hardly seeming to move with his lower lip. "I believe that so much harm has been done by previous policies that steps must be taken to nullify those policies as soon as possible. I believe, however, that nothing intemperate should be done."

The Vice-President for Space, Svengut Thorsen, struck the table twice in agreement, with a heavy palm.

"Absolutely," he boomed. "Absolutely right."

"My suggestion would be simple," Raphael Montresor said carefully. "We—the Board—must limit the President's capacity to expend money for programs that are of no—and I don't intend a pun—of no earthly use."

"Hear, hear," Svengut Thorsen said.

(In the vision screen room Ted Carr groaned, "They want to kill stockfare. They know that millions of extra shares have been printed and Montresor wants to kill any chance of our being able to use those shares in any way at all.")

The motion had passed over Waldemir Apfel's angry disagreement, "You will block the President in his capacity to make war, should that be necessary."

Montresor answered gently, "The current President of Earth Government wouldn't make war with any enthusiasm, having scrapped all our weapons. The argument is academic."

Apfel protested indignantly, "You will have forced Gavin Hew out of office, for all practical purposes, during a time of crisis."

Montresor nodded. "That is our intention, Mr. Apfel."

"How do you propose that the Board handle the matter of Earth's difficulties with the Rillut?"

(Matt, thinking that watching this visicast was like observing a tense chess match, noticed a movement at his side. The President had been handed a note and was

157

reading it, his craggy face expressionless.)

"I propose to take a firm position in this matter," Raphael Montresor was saying, his hands clasped tightly. "I propose to send a note to Emmi-to, the Rillut premier, informing him that Earth expects his people to conform to our standards or be banished from trading here. I have already notified Emmi-to that given a position of power in this government, I would do so."

"A reasonable stand," Basu said. "Firm, but certainly reasonable."

"It is warlike!" Apfel snorted. "The Rillut have their pride and they could only construe such a note as preliminary to a declaration of war, as amounting to threats. No, I say, no! And you must remember that the Rillut, too, have their militaristic crackpots who would welcome a war even if you just possibly might not."

Montresor overrode Apfel's protestations, saying smoothly, "I would suggest that the Board bring this matter to a vote and I hope that all in favor will raise their hands. The people watching from their vision screens should be able to see how the vote goes."

(Matt heard a door close softly in the vision screen room. Carr had whirled around before him and was already on his feet. "Where did the President go?" Carr asked.)

"One opposed, the balance, including myself, in favor," Basu said. "Thank you. The note will be sent out before the day is over. It is time for the Rillut to be made aware that they cannot interfere in Earth business on their own terms. Business is a two-way street, and the inj—"

Montresor suddenly turned away from the camera and Basu's glance followed him. The door to the visicast room had opened on Gavin Hew. The President of Earth Government walked in quietly, sparing only one glance for the renegades on his Board of Directors. He stared angrily at Montresor, who glared back. The others seemed to be holding their breath.

"I hope you've enjoyed this little game," Hew began. "The legality of your votes is certainly open to question, and I'm sure it's going to be questioned rigorously—and not just by me. But there are crucial matters to be decided now."

"I'm sure that the Board is aware of these matters," Montresor interjected.

Hew ignored him, which was probably a new experience for the multimillionaire.

"I have just been handed a message from Premier Emmi-to of the Rillut," Hew said, facing directly into the camera. "It seems that on receipt of a recent transmission from a wealthy Earthman with a vested interest in war—"

"I protest," Montresor began, but in vain.

"—the militaristic forces on his own planet have unilaterally decided to send Earth a reminder of their great power. A sonic bomb capable of killing hundreds of thousands of Earth people has been released without Premier Emmi-to's approval and is presently on its way toward Earth. It is expected to arrive within the hour." Gavin Hew probably surprised himself and every watcher by giving a sudden smile, wintry though it was. "And what do you plan to do about

159

that, Montresor?"

∞

When Matt heard the President's announcement, his first thought was: *I've got less than an hour to handle this.* He knew instinctively that he'd have to do the best he could and he'd have to take major responsibility on himself. It seemed as though he had spent his whole life in training for this one crisis. He knew his responses would have to be as swift as an android's and as dependable as a Mastro unit's; he would have to utilize his intelligence to the fullest.

Matt glanced at Lorene. The girl was surprisingly calm and in complete control of herself. "Come with me," Matt ordered, ignoring Ted Carr's baffled questions.

In his office at last, after an endless walk down a corridor devoid of other humans, he told the girl to make some visifon contacts and instructed her on exactly what to say.

Bulletins came to the office from a small transmitter and he glanced at them while waiting for Lorene to contact Siberia. The market was going haywire and tumbling frantically, but there was a surge in commodities. The poor were planning to demonstrate for more stockfare shares but statements had been given out that no more would be issued to them by the government. Matt was puzzled: if no more shares were going to be issued to the poor, why should Hew have authorized printing them? But now he had to move quickly. There was no time to lose.

His last contact was the briefest. He spoke to the man in charge of the vision screen transmission of the

160

Board of Directors meeting. "Blank it out," he ordered.

He broke contact, then turned to Lorene. Quietly they walked back to the vision screen room, where they found Ted Carr standing by the Mastro unit, gesturing furiously with one hand and pulling at toggles with the other.

"Nothing," he snapped. "These sets are out of order, every one of them."

"I gave the order," Matt said quietly. "There'll be no transmission to aid a sonic bomb's route."

"How is that really going to help?" Carr asked. "If the sound level is uniform, it's as if there wasn't any sound."

"I've got an idea about that," Matt said, glaring at his timepiece. "Come to my office and we'll find out if I'm right or wrong about this."

"Right about *what*, for Dow-Jones' sake?" Carr wanted to know. Matt made no added comment, but led the way down the hall.

Bulletins were chittering on freshly activated machines in Matt's office but none of the news was vital. The commodity market was out of all control and stocks could be picked up for a song. The streets were quiet, without cars or people moving. Lights had been turned out everywhere. Churches were open, but attendance was surprisingly light. A black leader had announced that black people forgave whites for their transgressions and that the Rillut were obviously practicing genocide against the black race. Sixteen thousand insurance policies had been cancelled in the last few minutes, and a group of bankers had announced a seminar on the prospects for their institutions for the future.

At a time when silence might be worth as much as life itself, Matt noticed wryly, dialogue went on and continued to be reported. He wondered if there was any moral justification for feeling wryly amused, then decided not to think about that.

He was staring glumly at the latest bulletins when the door opened on a grimly silent Gavin Hew. The President walked over to Matt, who stood courteously at his approach.

"Well?"

"I've closed off all vision screen transmission, Mr. President, so that there'll be silence, and I've arranged to try to deflect the bomb by—"

Another bulletin was coming over the machine. It said, ironically, that silence reigned on Earth. Electrical apparatus had by and large been closed down. Cars weren't being used. People waited in offices and homes and schools to find out where the sonic bomb would drop. Many were praying.

"What have you arranged for?" Hew asked, a muscle working in his jaw.

"I made one extra contact and asked for as much noise from that source as possible," Matt said. "I told the person I spoke to that the order had come directly from you, Mr. President."

"You've taken it on yourself to choose certain victims in a certain location, then." Hew drummed his fingers against their mates. "You've taken it on yourself to decide who lives and who dies—"

"No, sir," Matt said firmly. "Not if I'm right."

Another bulletin. Matt reached for this one without

162

permission. He wiped his brow after reading it, but the corners of his lips were stretched very slightly in the beginnings of a smile.

"I think we may have made it, sir," he said. "The sonic bomb has been sighted on a trajectory that must bring it toward Siberia."

"There are human beings living in Siberia, too."

"Yes, sir, but they've been hurried away from the noise center." He raised both hands placatingly before the President could ask another question. "You see, sir, the Vitaman plant is located there—the plant that Raphael Montresor owns most of, that makes the androids Montresor hopes to put into Earth jobs to make himself even more wealthy by adding to unemployment. If a war comes with the Rillut, the all-out war he wanted, there will be casualties among the able-bodies and Montresor will find it that much easier to put his androids to work afterward."

"He'd have to use an enormous number of androids to implement a scheme like that, besides which there are laws against the manufacture of androids past certain experimental levels."

"I submit, Mr. President, that Montresor has been breaking those laws. He located his plant at a distant point and has been manufacturing quantities of androids illegally—his recent behavior doesn't make any real sense to me, otherwise. If what the plant manager hinted is right, there must be half a million of them by now. In my opinion, he was deliberately understating the case when I spoke to him."

Carr, who had been staring aimlessly out the window, suddenly whirled around, his eyes narrowed shrewdly.

"So that's your pitch," he said softly. "The plant manager orders hundreds of thousands of androids in a distant area to make as much clatter as possible, and the sonic bomb homes in on those androids and causes no human casualties."

Matt nodded. "Whether I'm right or wrong, I can't know until—"

Another bulletin. Matt hesitated perceptibly, his eyes meeting the President's. It was Lorene Goldthwait, not afraid of the worst, who walked swiftly over to the little table and drew the bulletin from the machine. Hew took it from her hands, then looked down and read it. He tore the bulletin in half and then into quarters. His face was impassive.

He turned around to leave the office. At the door, he looked briefly at Matt, who was trying to catch his breath.

"Now I can resume negotiations with the Rillut," Hew said, and he smiled. "You did your job very well, Matt, very well indeed."

21

"... And so I am pleased to report that your Earth Government has reached an agreement with the planet Rillut. The agreement calls for Rillut and Earth to share the proceeds of trade on other planets and galaxies, so that neither Earth nor Rillut will take advantage of the other by an excess of merchandise and services placed. As for trade on each of our two planets, I am pleased to say that Rillut has agreed to liberalize its laws so that Earth traders can find a free market there. Now I suppose than many of you would like to know how this has been accomplished."

Hew paused. Although he must have appeared before vision screen cameras hundreds of times during his administration, he had never before appeared so buoyant and confident about the future.

"It was done in this way," Hew explained. "Your Earth Government decided to print an added billion shares of stockfare, as it has been called. In return for the ownership of those shares, the Rillut and Earth have come to their agreement. The value of the shares, and hence of the quarterly payment that goes to Rillut, will depend on the status and success of trade done by Earth firms. The shares entitled Earth to inquire rigorously into Rillut methods and to profit from the inquiries. The trade of the Rillut on Earth will therefore bring considerable profit to Earth Government as well, in part because the traders are aware that if the Rillut take advantage of Earth men from now on, they will be subtracting from their own eventual profits. I feel that what we have mainly purchased with our stockfare shares is the chance for a great merger of interests, a chance for Earth to fully learn from the great knowledge and talents and capacity of the Rillut."

Hew paused. "I feel that your Earth Government can look forward to a time of peace and prosperity perhaps unparalleled in our hist—"

∞

Matt, who had been watching in the vision screen room, was summoned back to his office for a visifon from Oscar Grayling. He walked along the noisy hallway with government workers chattering as usual and smiling at him when he passed, but he didn't see the smiles. He was upset at having been kept in the dark about Gavin Hew's plans for utilizing the newly printed stockfare shares that had been brought into existence in part through a half-joking suggestion of

166

his. Of course he had been too busy to ask about what had happened to the added shares, but he couldn't help thinking that he ought to have known, he ought to have been told.

He sat down behind his desk, and Oscar Grayling's features appeared on the visifon screen. The owner of Grayling's gave Matt a look of approval.

"You're a smart crew out there, all of you."

"Are you talking about the stockfare deal?" Matt shrugged instead of acknowledging praise to which he wasn't entitled.

"That and the business with Vitaman," Grayling added. "The deal with the Rillut is the smartest piece of work I've run across in a long time. All the people who say that a government can't be run on business principles, all those people ought to take a careful look at what Earth Government has just done."

"I suppose so."

Grayling chuckled. "So help me, it isn't every government that can head off a war by purchasing its own worst enemy, that can actually turn its worst enemy into a partly owned subsidiary, and do it without shedding a drop of blood. Yes, you're a clever bunch out there and I take my hat off to all of you."

22

Matt accepted the praise this time, having indeed helped Gavin Hew accomplish what had been done. The owner of Grayling's looked so cheerful and relaxed, for once, that Matt couldn't help commenting on it.

"Why not?" Oscar Grayling asked. "My father and my grandfather never played any part whatever in the saving of Earth or the making of such a colossal merger. I've contributed one of my key men and knowing that is enough to set me up, believe me."

Matt grinned. If Oscar Grayling wanted to believe that he had been a major factor in the new arrangement with the Rillut and he felt better as a result, Matt certainly didn't mind.

Grayling asked, "When are you coming back to work

for me, Matt? The crisis seems to be over."

"In government, something else always comes up."

"Maybe so, but the job I've got to offer you is a lot easier than what you've been doing for Earth Government."

Matt said carefully, "I think I ought to stay, Mr. G. Besides, I hear that Ned Jackler is doing very well on my old job, and I owe him the chance to make his mark at it."

"Good luck," Grayling said, surprising Matt by one of the very few completely personal remarks Matt had ever heard from him, and the first he could remember that had ever been addressed to Matt Brisbane. It was as if he had graduated at last from a particularly difficult school.

"Thank you, Mr. G.," Matt said.

"Oscar. You can call me Oscar now."

"Thank you, Oscar," Matt said, and broke the contact. He felt stunned.

∞

"Good afternoon, gentlemen," Gavin Hew said, getting to his feet, "and thank you."

The members of the new Board of Directors left the room slowly. Hew had replaced the Board members who had betrayed him and had enlarged it, adding a number of new men to the group. No longer would a man with Raphael Montresor's former wealth seriously consider trying to bribe them all.

Matt walked into the room as the door opened, surprised to find himself the target for a number of quizzical and almost hostile looks from Board members on their way out.

Gavin Hew smiled at him, though, and said, "I think we've got the ball rolling now, Matt. I've put in a new Vice-President whose job it's going to be to nourish competition in business."

Matt, who didn't often talk to the President about legislative plans, said, "You'll have to break up a few businesses."

"Yes, we plan to try to break up firms in industries where four suppliers make up more than fifty percent of the market or eight firms make up more than seventy percent."

"There'll be a number of new mergers in that case, you know."

"I hope to be able to put through a bylaw banning further mergers by the top five hundred corporations unless they unload assets equal to what they'd gain in a merger."

"A firm could still use its assets to raise the devil, Mr. President. It's only fair to say so."

"I hope to put a limit of two billion dollars on the assets of any corporation."

Matt shook his head. "You'd have to raise your limits for utilities, I think."

"Utilities and other rate-regulated industries," Hew agreed. "Yes, I think so. If we can put that program through, Matt, we'll have accomplished something vital to the future of Earth."

"I'll be glad to help, sir," Matt said as he followed the President back to his airy office.

"You've helped already," Hew assured him, smiling. "The Board members who don't like the idea have been allowed to get the impression that you, with your business experience, thought of putting what they consider shackles on business."

"Me?" Matt remembered the few dirty looks he'd received and shook his head wonderingly. "As if making a business more trimly efficient is the same as shackling it."

"Business always finds ways to profit from regulation," Hew agreed. "Ways that are legal and ways that aren't. So-called business leaders, though, have got to whine as they cheat and take advantage, then go home to complain to their families about those freeloaders who are on stockfare."

"*Were* on stockfare, you mean, Mr. President. What with the added shares, the originals are worth very little in such wide distribution. The poor and unemployed saved the day for Earth and big business, Mr. President. What are we going to do to help them now?"

Hew sat down behind his desk at last and absently touched the button of his desk scanner. "The market is rising solidly for just about the first time since Montresor and Skene decided to try to take over the government of Earth. Montresor is still a potential menace, I suppose, but it'll be a while before he can get the resources together to make another try for this chair of mine."

There was a rap on the door and Ted Carr and Lorene Goldthwait entered. Matt, emboldened, asked again: "What's to become of the poor and unemployed now, Mr. President?"

Hew replied softly, taking time to frame his answer carefully, "We have to try to help them again, but in a

171

more imaginative and effective way. We have to put them into a position where those who want to help themselves can do it, but we have to realize that there will always be those who would rather live off the people who work. If the allowance credits are increased for every child, then there will always be poor people who will give birth to more children to take advantage of the added allowance. You have to agree—and I think that our experience with stockfare would prove the point—that not all the poor and unemployed are people who only want a chance to join the middle class. Many of them have known only poverty and are only at ease or in balance as part of a poverty situation. They see any offer of help as a chance to take advantage of them. We might as well admit that the poor are human beings with all the mental and emotional disadv—"

"Does that justify not making a move to help them?" Matt asked angrily. "I wouldn't want to be part of a government whose chief executive felt that way."

Lorene gasped.

Hew answered, "All it means is that Earth Government's strategy toward the poor and unemployed needs to be carefully rethought, and we all have to start from scratch on a new program."

Matt rubbed his strong chin with a hand, then said carefully, "I didn't mean to sound like a prig, Mr. President."

"I suppose that your job has been getting to you," the President answered placatingly. "After all, no one else on the top level of government has to deal with so many different people and interest in conflict. Maybe what you need is a change."

Matt winced. Just when he felt sure he had learned the ins and outs of the most murderously difficult job in government, the President had decided to ditch him.

"I'll have my resignation on your desk in the morning, Mr. President."

"Dammit, no!" Hew thumped a strong fist solidly on a section of the oval desk. "I want to have you working close to me, Matt. But Ted Carr can take your place here and I can give Brubaker the job of Vice-President for Disadvantaged Aid—a change in the department's name might be helpful—and send you on a special mission. Yes, I really think I have to do that."

Carr turned excitedly to Matt. "The President wanted me here to tell you that but he beat me to it. So many people are going to be sure you originated the President's business reform policy that you'll be more effective for a while in a different slot. Believe me, this is as much for your good as for the President's."

Matt reluctantly nodded his agreement.

Hew broke in, "I want to send you to Rillut, Matt. You'll help coordinate their ties with Earth. It's not a makework job, believe me. There are great difficulties. The militant forces on Rillut are opposed to the stock deal and might make trouble. You're going to have to walk a very narrow path, I'm afraid. You might even live under a state of siege at times, like people in the Rillut delegation to Earth have done on occasion. In a sense, Matt, I'm sending you to the frontier."

Matt nodded slowly. He remembered Yoru-ko and the hostility the Rillut had encountered on Earth.

"I think you'll avoid the obvious traps, though, and I expect you to make a number of contacts that will be

173

useful in the future."

Matt said, "I'll need people to come with me, Mr. President."

"Eight representatives from Earth are already stationed on Rillut," Hew answered, then paused. "But you might be well advised to take another dozen people with you."

Matt glanced toward Lorene, then asked, "May I take Miss Goldthwait as my personal secretary?"

"Of course," Hew agreed. "She'll be missed," he added gallantly.

Matt shook hands with the President and left the room with Lorene. In the cool corridor, Lorene's hazel eyes glistened moistly.

"I won't be coquettish and complain that you haven't asked me if I want to go," she said quietly. "You want me to be part of the mission so of course I agree."

"I asked for your company because you and I are used to each other. It'll be easier to work together."

"Of course, Matt." Was she laughing at him now? "There couldn't be anything personal in it."

"I don't think we'll see too much of one another," Matt said quickly. "I'll be on a backbreaking schedule, from what I can gather."

"I'm sure that's true," Lorene said, smiling, "but you haven't arranged spaceship accommodations as often as I've had to do, so you don't know that the trip to Rillut takes eight months, Matt."

"That's a long time," he said thoughtfully.

"In eight months we might get to know each other so well that we may want to spend more time together on Rillut than we might do otherwise. And I believe

174

there'll be a chaplain on the ship, in case we want to use one of his services—"

"It'll be a long time before we make any decision like that."

"Of course it will, but we're going to see so much of one another on the ship that we can consult about it pretty often."

Matt smiled. "We're probably going to be grateful for a long rest once the mission reaches Rillut."

"Well, you know the old saying, Matt: getting there is half the fun."

He laughed joyously now and put an arm around her slim waist as they walked out of Government Headquarters and into the warm September afternoon.

www.ingramcontent.com/pod-product-compliance
Lightning Source LLC
Chambersburg PA
CBHW022155260626
47155CB00018B/1933